# WHO WAS CALLING ME AT THIS HOUR?

"Cat Woman? Hello, are you there?"

"Rothwax? Lieutenant Rothwax, is this you? Why on earth are you calling me at three-thirty in the morning?"

"What does time matter to a prowling feline spirit like yourself? Anyway, I'm *Mister* Rothwax now. Got a new job as director of security for the Korean Merchants Association."

"I think you're calling because you need help."

"Somebody does. But it ain't me. I just got a call from your boyfriend, Anthony."

"*Basillio?*"

"Right. He's being held for questioning by Manhattan North detectives."

"Questioning for what?"

"A murder . . . "

# A CAT IN FINE STYLE

*An Alice Nestleton Mystery*

## Lydia Adamson

A SIGNET BOOK

SIGNET
Published by the Penguin Group
Penguin Books USA Inc., 375 Hudson Street,
New York, New York 10014, U.S.A.
Penguin Books Ltd, 27 Wrights Lane,
London W8 5TZ, England
Penguin Books Australia Ltd, Ringwood,
Victoria, Australia
Penguin Books Canada Ltd, 10 Alcorn Avenue,
Toronto, Ontario, Canada M4V 3B2
Penguin Books (N.Z.) Ltd, 182–190 Wairau Road,
Auckland 10, New Zealand

Penguin Books Ltd, Registered Offices:
Harmondsworth, Middlesex, England

First published by Signet, an imprint of Dutton Signet,
a division of Penguin Books USA Inc.

First Printing, November, 1995
10 9 8 7 6 5 4 3 2 1

The first chapter of this book appeared in *A Cat on a Winning Streak*,
the tenth volume in this series.
Cover art by Robert Crawford

 REGISTERED TRADEMARK—MARCA REGISTRADA

Printed in the United States of America

PUBLISHER'S NOTE
This is a work of fiction. Names, characters, places, and incidents
either are the product of the author's imagination or are used
fictitiously, and any resemblance to actual persons, living or dead,
events, or locales is entirely coincidental.

BOOKS ARE AVAILABLE AT QUANTITY DISCOUNTS WHEN USED TO PROMOTE
PRODUCTS OR SERVICES. FOR INFORMATION PLEASE WRITE TO PREMIUM
MARKETING DIVISION, PENGUIN BOOKS USA INC., 375 HUDSON STREET, NEW YORK,
NEW YORK 10014.

# Chapter 1

"This is nuts," Basillio said, rubbing his hands together. "I don't know why *I'm* getting so nervous. I'm not the one doing this stupid thing."

"Maybe Tony's right, Aunt Alice. I feel very foolish."

The paint-flecked doors of the rickety old elevator slammed shut behind us.

So, both my niece and my friend Tony Basillio thought this venture was silly. What could I say? It wasn't easy to think of a defense for it.

Alison and I were going to be part of a fashion spread, odd as that sounds. There was a theme to the layout: different generations of photogenic women modeling original fashions by two trendy downtown *couturieres*. There would be mothers and daughters in matching ball gowns, grandmothers and granddaughters in silk baseball jackets. That sort of thing.

And then there would be Alison and me—

wearing identical scanty camisoles. It was all part of the lingerie-as-daywear craze.

Foolish? Well, I suppose I did feel a little foolish. But we were being offered unbelievably good pay for a couple of days work, and I'd been through the torture of losing twelve pounds for the camera. So I wasn't about to get back on that infernal elevator and go home.

Grace Ann and Samantha Collins, the two fashion-designer sisters who had recently hit it big in the fashion world, had once been my cat-sitting clients. They had operated a little boutique in Chelsea for years, selling their hand-loomed woolens and exquisite silk scarves and impeccably tailored working women's skirts to a very loyal and very discriminating clientele, but a limited one. I myself treasure the one and only Collins-made item I've ever owned: a long velvet skirt of midnight blue, which I received as a Christmas gift one year from a friend whose husband's death had left her with more money than sense, and to whom the act of shopping had become life itself.

The talented Collins sisters went on for years just managing to make ends meet— just. And then, for whatever reason, or possibly for no reason whatever, Boutique Ariel (so named because Ariel had been their mother's name) and the two sisters behind it caught fire. In the past year or so, they'd designed the wedding gowns of more than two dozen high-profile New York brides. They were being featured in all the "important" industry publications and their clothing was turning up at A-list gatherings at A-list restaurants on the backs of A-list celebrities.

Now, what in God's name did this world of society brides and gossip columns and *Harper's Bazaar* spreads have to do with me? Nothing. Absolutely nothing. So when Grace Ann Collins phoned me one day about a month ago, I assumed she needed me to look after Bobbin, the big blue point Himalayan cat I'd had so much fun with a couple of years ago while the sisters were on a buying trip in Savannah.

But no. What Grace Ann wanted was to photograph me! She and Samantha were promoting an extensive line of underwear-inspired fashions that were all the rage among the trend-conscious young—and the not so young.

"As far as fashion goes, Alice," she had said, "you are well nigh hopeless. It's your milky white skin that interests us. And your torso. And your marvelous long legs of course. I just know you're going to be fabulous in those airy little things of ours. And really, honey, what woman wouldn't want to be shot by Fliss?"

"Fliss? What is that—a bug spray?"

"Fliss Francis! Fliss Francis!" had been her incredulous reply. Did I mean to say I'd never heard of the award-winning British photographer? The one who was going to immortalize me, Grace Ann promised.

Alice Nestleton, fashion model. It was absurd, obviously, and I was on the verge of telling her so. But then she named a ballpark figure for the fee I'd receive for this assignment. I said I'd think it over.

Grace Ann phoned me again three days later. She and Samantha had their hearts set on having me as a model, torso and all. And the price had gone up. Before the conversation was over, I'd given her my niece's phone number as well. Alison, at least, had heard of Fliss Francis.

And that is how we came to be in this lovely renovated cast-iron building on Greene Street—well, everything but the nerve-rattling elevator had been renovated. Today's photo session was taking place in a glamorous ShHo loft belonging to someone named Niles Wiegel, who, to the best of my knowledge, was neither artist nor photographer nor designer nor Indian chief. He was simply someone with money whom other people with money knew. That sort of thing isn't exclusive to SoHo, I guess, but it surely seemed that way.

The door to the loft apartment swung open to reveal a hive of activity. In fact, the scene was not unlike the backstage atmosphere in a theater a few days before opening. There were lights and flats and wardrobe racks and cartons stacked or stashed or flung here and there. Half a dozen people moved frantically about the apartment, to no apparent purpose.

I spotted Samantha Collins, knee-deep in chiffon, peering critically at a spaghetti-strap nightgown on a puffy satin hanger.

Samantha and Grace Ann were both lovely, smart women. Both in their early fifties, both looking younger than that, both reed-thin. Both dyed-in-the-wool New Yorkers born in Mississippi and raised in genteel poverty by an ambitious iron butterfly of a mother from one of those mythic "good" southern families.

But where Grace Ann was independent, garrulous, and shrewd—a kind of modern-day belle—her sister Samantha worked more behind the scenes. She did a great deal of the seamstressing work and took her pleasure not in lunching with fashion magazine editors but in tending the impressive garden behind the first-floor apartment of the brownstone the two had shared for some twenty-five years.

"Alice, Alice, Alice!" I heard my name repeated in a barely perceptible southern drawl.

Grace Ann, in a perfect black knit jumper, white shirt, and antique high-button boots, came floating toward us. She kissed me lightly on each cheek, then bestowed the same blessing on Alison.

"Grace Ann," I said, "this is my . . . this is Tony Basillio."

"My, aren't you handsome!" she said immediately.

Tony cleared his throat and took her hand.

"I hope it's all right that I brought Tony along. He was inordinately curious and I didn't think anyone would mind."

"Of course not. We can always make use of a strong back."

Alison smirked.

"Fliss isn't here yet," Grace Ann said. "I can't abide tardiness, can you? Except in a genius, of course. Come along now and meet the others."

Samantha had noticed us by then and waved distractedly in our direction.

A thin man dressed all in black cashmere, about thirty-five years old, flew through the room then, calling his hellos over one shoulder. He was carrying a pitcher of tomato juice.

"That was Niles," Grace Ann pronounced. "He and Lainie were good enough to let us invade their home for the day. Which brings me to—"

Grace Ann broke off then and turned to grasp the hand of the tall man in impeccably fitted jeans who had walked up behind her.

"—which brings me to my lovely friend

Hector. Hector Naciemento. He and Niles are old friends."

It was obvious from the way she interlaced her fingers with his and looked up into his liquid eyes that the two of them were more than "lovely" friends. Well well well—as my grandmother used to say when something juicy was told to her—so Grace Ann had a young lover.

Hector was a sublimely beautiful man with huge, transporting eyes the color of espresso and flawless, tanned skin. The pushed-up sleeves of his white sweatshirt set off the muscles in his upper arms like sapphires around the star diamond in a lady's brooch. Alison turned on a 14-karat smile as he caressed her hand in greeting. Tony seemed almost embarrassed, looking down at the floor as he shook hands. Hector murmured something to me about having been told how lovely I was, but, frankly, I wasn't really listening. There was something almost hypnotic about his good looks.

"And this is Penny Motion," I heard Grace Ann say. "She'll be helping with your makeup."

Penny Motion might have been as attractive an exemplar of young female beauty as Hector was of masculine good looks. But the picture she presented undercut that severely. Her skin was powdered to give the effect of library paste, her wonderful light green eyes seemed buried in the crudely drawn black lines around them, and her lipstick was a ghastly purplish black. Her jeans were more tatters than fabric, and on her feet were laceless combat boots that looked as if they'd seen active duty in at least two long wars.

Penny nodded curtly at the three of us and plopped a heavy case into Hector's arms. He smiled indulgently at her and then followed her over to a desk in the corner of the room.

"Can I get anyone a Bloody Mary?"

The speaker was a pleasant-looking woman, barely thirty years old, I'd say, also dressed in severe SoHo black, with auburn hair pulled back into a ponytail.

"Hi, I'm Lainie Wiegel," she said. "Exciting, isn't it? Is everybody stoked for Fliss?"

Before I could answer, Samantha Collins stepped up and took my arm. "All right, Alice, Alison, let's see what we have here."

That was her way of saying it was time for us to change. She took a ruffled bed jacket and held it up to Alison's face, as if assessing the appropriateness of the color for my niece.

Tony alone accepted Lainie's offer of a drink. I watched them disappear into the kitchen area.

Samantha busied herself undoing the zipper of my drab corduroy dress. "Well, dear," she said, "let's have a look at you. Hmm.

Haven't you lost just *pounds and pounds* of weight? . . . Oh . . . No, you haven't."

I laughed in spite of the insult. "I did my best, Samantha."

"I'm sure you'll be just fine. At least you know how to walk and how to stand still. You're an actress. Oh, Alice, you know Sidney, don't you?"

Standing in my slip, I looked over at the late-middle-age man in wire-rim glasses who was handing Samantha a scissor. "No," I said simply.

"No? I was sure you'd met. Well, Alice, this is our attorney, Sidney Rickover. Sidney, this is Alice Nestleton."

"A pleasure," Mr. Rickover said and quickly backed away from my seminakedness. I noticed how carefully he lifted his feet and set them down again, as if afraid to make a noise. Where had Sidney come from? He had to have been in the loft all along, but I had never even noticed him.

"And this is Alison Chevigny," Samantha added. "Isn't she adorable?"

Sidney Rickover's smiled indicated that if Samantha thought she was, then he thought she was.

"Samantha, I think that covers just about everything," he said. "If you'll sign all three copies of those papers—"

"Yes, Sidney, we'll get to it today, I promise."

Mr. Rickover leaned forward slightly as if

to kiss Samantha's cheek, but at that very moment she turned back to me.

"Good-bye, Sidney," she said,.

"Oh no, Sidney! You mustn't leave yet." That was Grace Ann, who had joined us. "You must go over that lease, Sidney. I've got a half-dozen questions you simply must answer before I can even *think* about signing."

"Of course, Grace Ann."

With that, the two of them walked off.

From time to time Basillio popped up here and there in the loft. I heard Niles explaining to him how the computer worked. A few minutes later I spotted Basillio toting lighting equipment under the supervision of Penny Motion, who barked out directions as they made their way across the floor. Then I thought I heard him lecturing Lainie on the proper way to steam milk for cappuccino. Only once did I catch him peering behind the screen and into the makeshift dressing room that Samantha had set up for Alison and me.

This was like a rehearsal that had no payoff. No opening night, no performance. Just an endless rehearsal. I was growing tired of Samantha's ministrations and impatient with Penny's ongoing application of paint to my face. It was especially disturbing that I couldn't see what she was doing to me. I kept thinking that perhaps she wanted to make me over in her own spooky image.

I saw Alison regarding herself in the free-standing, full-length mirror. She looked part waif and part sex kitten in her pink cami-sole. There was an expression on her face I couldn't quite decipher. Was she pleased with herself or was she appalled at what she'd gotten herself into?

What *I'd* gotten her into—that was the truth of it. As the day wore on, I became increasingly ashamed of having involved her in this ridiculous enterprise. I wondered if Felix, my niece's older and very paternal lover, would hold this against me forever.

The heady aroma of Italian roast coffee filled the loft. I changed into a robe and went to get a cup. After I'd had my little break, I went off in search of the bathroom.

Lord, I got a terrible scare when I pulled open the sliding door to the bedroom at the rear of the loft!

It was as if a fur coat had come to life and was preparing to ravage me.

Jumping from the high loft bed, straight at me, was Bobbin! Humongous blue Bobbin, who seemed to be the size of a pony.

"God, Bobbin! You scared the daylights out of me."

The big ball of fur rubbed against my ankles. I leaned down and roughed him up a bit.

"That's right, you old bear. It's me, Alice. What are you doing in this place?"

Bobbin seemed to bristle at the question.

He drew himself up haughtily and retreated behind the armoire.

When I rejoined the group, Niles and Lainie were winding their way around the room, offering trays of sandwiches and snacks to the others. Tony came bounding up to me.

"Swede, I have to admit I thought this was going to be another one of your debacles. But it's great!"

"Oh, you think so, do you, Tony?"

"Yeah. I mean," he dropped his voice a little then, "I thought these people were going to be downtown pinheads—too much money and no esthetics. But they're nice. Except for that weird-looking girl, I mean. But she's kind of interesting too. Kind of subverbal. Lainie was a theater major at Bennington, did you know that? And listen, how come you don't wear things like that all the time?" He pointed to the sheer spaghetti strap gown Samantha had been examining earlier.

"Probably for the same reason you don't wear things like that all the time, Tony."

"Come on, loosen up, Swede. I think it's going pretty well. Let me get you a sandwich. That guy Niles just made his special paté in that . . . that thing . . . that blender thing."

"No sandwiches for me. I don't want to get one of those looks from Samantha. I just want that photographer to get here so I can put this all behind me."

Samantha helped Alison and me into matching plain white muslin slips, then ice blue bias-cut nightgowns, then yellow boxer shorts.

Penny Motion was good at her job. She made us look like Times Square hookers and then, with the help of a couple of old-fashioned hair rollers, like sex-starved trailer park housewives; she even made us up to look as though we were wearing no makeup at all.

And still Fliss Francis, the tardy genius, did not arrive. At one o'clock I broke down and went into the kitchen looking for left-over paté.

Niles Wiegel was seated on a kitchen stool in front of, as Tony had called it, that blender thing. He was whipping up another one of his specialties, no doubt.

"I was wondering," I said, "if there's anything left to eat. I don't care about my cheekbones anymore."

Niles said nothing. In fact, there was no sign he'd heard me come in.

I spoke more loudly this time. "Excuse me, Niles."

He remained perfectly still. His profile was oddly cast.

I walked over to the counter. Niles's right hand was resting on the control panel of the Cuisinart. I tapped him once on the shoulder and he slid easily off his seat, like fine

Chinese silk, not stopping until he hit the tiled floor. Very hard.

Oh my. I stepped back, suddenly cold.

"I think you'd better come in here," I called into the other room.

"Who?" Grace Ann answered back.

"All of you."

I heard Lainie Wiegel scream.

Tony sighed heavily. And I think he uttered a curse.

Hector Naciemento and Sidney Rickover rushed over to the motionless body.

Sidney reached down into Niles's black T-shirt, groping for a pulse at the side of his neck.

"He's . . . There's no . . . He's dead," the attorney said.

Lainie cried out again and fell into Grace Ann's arms.

Samantha covered her mouth with both hands.

"What shall we do?" asked Hector softly.

"Call somebody?" Penny suggested.

I felt Alison's fingers around my wrist. She was hurting me. I gently guided her backward, into Tony's hold.

Just then there was a commotion at the front door. "Hello! Hey, Niles? Anyone home?"

Fliss Francis had arrived at last.

# Chapter 2

There was a knock at my door.

Crazy Pancho heard it, too. And went scampering toward the water heater. Bushy couldn't be bothered. He was too busy with his nail-sharpening exercises.

I made a quick survey of the room. Well, I guess it would have to do. The cat toys and the opened, half-read magazines and catalogs looked more like props than clutter, I hoped.

Grace Ann Collins, who had called less than an hour ago and asked if I could possibly make time to see her that afternoon, was smiling when I opened the door. She carried a thin, flat parcel wrapped in dyed parchment paper and decorated with a grosgrain ribbon of mossy green.

"Dear, dear Alice. Just look at you in your new surroundings! What a charming place it is!"

"Why, thank you, Grace Ann. We certainly do love it."

Every conversation with Grace Ann

turned into a series of old Savannah platitudes. I always ended up sounding exactly like her. No one knew who was fooling whom.

"Why, goodness yes. So much . . . potential . . . for charm."

"May I take your coat, Grace Ann?"

"Thank you, dear. Oh. Here's a little something for you."

The little something was a square of exquisite silk with my initials in tiny letters in the left corner. These scarves had been selling well, Grace Ann told me, and Julia, the sales assistant at the boutique, really enjoyed personalizing them with her "sweet little embroidering skills."

I took Grace Ann on the two-cent tour of my loft, bragged about my view. She was polite of course—Grace Ann wouldn't forget her manners at her own hanging—but I got the feeling she wasn't paying a great deal of attention to the high ceilings or my description of the tile work I planned to have done in the bathroom.

Bushy had spruced himself up and was now all but begging Grace Ann to admire him. She barely noticed him though, leaning down only once to give him a distracted scratch behind the ear.

As Grace Ann and I settled back—me with my apple juice, she with her cup of tea—her face took on a look of out-and-out worry.

"Alice, frankly, these past few days have been just about the most trying of my life."

"Yes. I can imagine. It was terrible, what happened that day. So sudden. And he was such a young man."

"Of course, it's the roughest on poor Hector. He and Niles were such close friends."

What about his wife, you fool? I thought. But when I spoke, I asked: "How *is* Hector?"

"Just beside himself. Absolutely beside himself. And now, so am I."

"What do you mean?"

"The autopsy's come through."

"What did it show?"

"Sudden heart attack. Brought on by the ingestion of something to which he was violently allergic: almonds. They called it acute something or other poison. He apparently had a deadly allergy to almonds. And it turns out the paté he'd eaten was riddled with them—it was full of almond paste."

"But Niles made that paté himself, didn't he?"

"Precisely the point, Alice."

"God, what a terrible mistake to make. It's grotesque."

"My opinion exactly, honey. But the authorities don't see it that way. Not yet, anyway. They say they aren't calling Niles's death an accident."

"What? Do you mean they think someone added the almond paste deliberately—to hurt him—kill him?"

"They won't say so, but obviously they haven't ruled it out. The case remains open for the moment, they say. Neither one way nor the other. Neither this nor that. And no amount of talking seems to dissuade them."

"I'm sorry."

"It's horrible, I tell you. And ridiculous!"

I wanted to assure Grace Ann that I understood, that I knew it was ridiculous to think any of Niles's friends could've wanted to kill him. But I didn't say anything. I'd given up predicting what people would or would not do to one another.

I stared into my apple juice. For some reason, the possibility of death by doctored paté seemed so much worse than death by gunshot or stabbing or hanging. The banality of it was insufferable.

Grace Ann stood up suddenly.

"Oh, Alice, I know what a dreadfully selfish person it makes me seem, but, while this mess over Niles goes on, we can't seem to accomplish anything. Between the police questioning and Hector's upset and poor Lainie . . . well, I don't know. It's as though they've all fallen apart. Even Samantha. I never dreamed it would affect her this way, but she's just as paralyzed as Hector now. We're at a critical time with the business, you know—shipping deadlines to meet, the ads, another wedding—and they've all just . . . let go."

"I'm sure everyone will come through it all

right," I said, "when the shock of Niles's death wears off." I had to hope those clichéd words were comfort enough for Grace Ann. Why, in fact, did I always try to comfort people?

She began shaking her head resolutely, mumbling to herself. "Maybe they think I'm a heartless bitch, but I can't fall apart, too. I can't let go, too. Someone simply *has* to carry on." She looked at me pleadingly. "Do you understand me, Alice? Do you?"

I did, and I didn't. But what I said was, "Of course."

"Good. I'm so happy that you do. Because I've come to make sure that you'll be able to continue with the work we started the minute Fliss can reschedule."

I stared blankly at her for a few seconds. It took me that long to realize that she meant she expected me to get back into those lacy, expensive getups and have my photo taken. That I had to allow Penny Motion to slather that makeup all over me again. It was strange how easily I'd forgotten about all that. The sudden, awful death of Niles Wiegel had erased it all.

"Oh," I said, sounding dumb, "well—"

"Please, Alice! You don't mean to say you've taken on another commitment?"

"No."

She sat down again.

"Thank goodness for that at least." Grace Ann set her teacup aside and undid the clasp on her handbag. "Honey, would you call the police if I had just one cigarette?"

"Help yourself, Grace Ann." I pushed a saucer her way.

"What a relief," she said.

I didn't know whether she meant the first puff of her cigarette or my telling her I had made no other commitments. Commitment to what? I hadn't had a job offer in months. God knows, the modeling job was the last kind of commitment I wanted to make. I thought back to how foolish I felt in that white muslin teddy, and recalled the unreadable look on Alison's face as she watched herself in the mirror.

But, all that aside, I needed that money, and the few hours' work I'd done on the day of Niles's death was only going to bring a fraction of the fee I'd been promised for the job. Sure, I needed the money. But the wolf was hardly at my door. My landlord, who happened to be my niece Alison's lover, was all but paying *me* to live in his building. What the modeling money could mean was the difference between a winter with old boots and that paper-thin chenille thing I threw across my bed, or a winter with new Manolo Blahniks and the delicious-looking down comforter in the shop window up Hudson Street.

Besides, it would be doubly hard to say no to Grace Ann and Samantha at a time like this—when they obviously needed all the help they could get. When they obviously needed their friends. Over and above the shock of Niles's death, this was, as Grace Ann had told me, a critical time for the business.

"I suppose," I said halfheartedly, "I should call my niece to make sure there's room in her schedule."

"Alison's told me she'll be waiting for our call. Hasn't a thing to do, she said. What a sweet child she is. Oh! and those bones."

"I know."

After she left, I drank the rest of my juice. It tasted faintly of almonds. I shivered. Then I burst into laughter, because my Maine coon was posing again—this time by the door—sitting up very straight in his very best "Am I not the most exquisite feline you have ever laid eyes on?" pose.

# Chapter 3

The ceremony took place in a sedate gray stone chapel on West 19th Street. It was brief and the mourners had turned out in fairly large numbers. So I was told. Niles Wiegel was buried in a family plot somewhere in Queens. So I was told. I attended neither the funeral nor the burial, but I did send flowers.

Yes, I had agreed to go back and resume the fashion shoot whenever Fliss Francis was ready, but I wasn't just sitting by the phone, waiting for the call from the Collins sisters. I was sending out feelers about acting jobs. So far, the field looked utterly frozen.

To some minds, an actor without a script is not an actor. What about a cat-sitter without a cat to sit for? Currently I had no clients. I don't know why, but I felt the urgent need to have a job of some sort, right away.

I'd just finished an assignment that took me to Brooklyn Heights every day. I was taking care of a special elderly cat, Brownie, who had long ago gone blind and now had the look of an ancient oracle. Brownie could nose her way through my bag and snout out the catnip mouse faster than any feline I'd ever known. But now the Shipmans were home from their holiday in Florence. I was kind of sad about it.

Tony Basillio was out of work, too. But not altogether impoverished. And not homeless, either, because he'd moved into the East Side apartment where I'd been living before moving to my West Village loft. Luckily, the summer had brought Tony steady work; he'd earned a fat fee for consulting work with a new experimental theater troupe that had a generous endowment; and, not the least explanation for Tony's solvency, he'd won several hundred dollars at an outing to Belmont Raceway with an old actor friend of ours.

Spending time with Basillio often made me feel as if I were a kid playing hooky. He and I had been going to a lot of museums lately. And to a lot of hole-in-the-hole-in-the-wall productions of one-act plays considered revolutionary in the 1960s. And afternoon movies. Even an outdoor charity basketball game.

And, Basillio being Basillio, he was showing up at my place some afternoons with plans that didn't require us to leave the apartment at all.

It was all pleasant enough, but, in my opinion, we both needed a job.

We walked for miles that autumn afternoon. I wasn't in the mood to talk much, but I needn't have worried. Tony was unusually talkative—even for Tony—expounding on the eclipse of Brecht and its ramifications for stage designers everywhere.

We'd taken some sandwiches into Central Park and then strolled to a revival house— one of the last two in Manhattan, I believe— where we saw an old French thriller, *The Sleeping Car Murders*, with Montand and Signoret and Trintignant.

By the time we arrived back at the loft, it was early evening. I was exhausted. But Tony still had energy to burn. After I made coffee, he finally stopped his all-day monologue and his amorous side overshadowed the loquacious side.

We stood kissing in the kitchen for a while.

We were just drawing the curtain across the huge window near my bed when the telephone rang.

"Don't pick it up, Swede," Tony warned.

"All right. I'll let the thing get it."

I kicked out of my shoes, listening to my own voice on the answering machine recording. Then came the beep. Then nothing. At least, not for a couple of seconds.

Basillio and I both stood listening, waiting for the caller to say something. I held one shoe in my hand. He was holding the dust mop, the long handle of which we'd been using to reach up to the top of the window and pull the curtain shut.

When the caller finally spoke, it was through tears.

"Hello. Hello, Miss Nestleton. Please. This is Lainie Wiegel. I need to see you as soon as possible. Listen, Miss Nestleton. If you're there, please pick up. I . . . I'm sorry . . . Really, I'm sorry . . . but I just don't know what else to do." Her voice broke into sobs then.

Tony sighed. "Oh boy."

"Yes. I couldn't have put it better," I said.

Tony hefted the dust mop and dragged its handle across the curtain rod, once more admitting the charmed evening light.

I was not happy to be back on the street again. For any reason. But Lainie had been only a breath away from hysteria. There was no way I could have in good conscience refused to come over to see her.

I could read it in Basillio's eyes: I had allowed Lainie to ruin the evening of lovemaking (and talk, no doubt) he'd been looking forward to. But I knew he wouldn't stay mad at me for long.

"Come, come, Basillio," I said soothingly as we crossed Sixth Avenue. "You just be patient. And when we get home, we'll see if we can't locate that black scarf you're so fond of. And those patent leather heels."

"That's very funny, Swede. But it reminds me of something."

"What?"

"How come you're so seldom funny?"

"I beg your pardon?"

"How come you don't make more jokes? I mean, it's not that you don't have a sense of humor."

"Tony, anyone who's been friends with you for as long as I have must have a sense of humor."

He shrugged.

We turned onto Greene Street and found the building with the perilous old elevator. I rang for it, just the way I'd done on the day of the aborted fashion shoot. At long last the thing arrived. When the elevator finally opened, Lainie Wiegel herself was on it.

Her face was terribly puffy. She was all cried out, I hoped.

Once inside the loft, she began to speak to us, her voice appearing to gain normalcy, strength with every word.

"You've probably heard from one of the Collinses by now that the police think Niles's death might have been an accident or might have been caused deliberately."

"Yes," I said. "Grace Ann told me."

"Well, I frankly don't give a damn what the police say. I know which one it was."

"Grace Ann feels the same way."

Lainie laughed bitterly. "Oh, I doubt that."

"What do you mean? She told me she thought the notion that one of the people here could have killed Niles is ridiculous."

"Yes," Lainie said. "She would say that. And I say that to believe anything *other* than that is ridiculous."

"In other words, you're sure that someone did kill him."

"Yes! Yes! I know it like I know my own name. What do you think Niles was—crazy? A fool? He had had an allergy to almonds since he was a baby. That's what he told me while we were on our honeymoon. The waiter offered us a fancy dessert with almonds and Niles almost turned blue."

I shot an exasperated look in Tony's direction, but he had turned his head. He was looking at the liquor cabinet.

"Please forgive me," Lainie said sincerely. "Both of you. I just seem to have let go of everything. Please let me offer you a drink."

I said no, thanks.

Basillio stepped toward the cabinet. "It's all right," he said to Lainie. "You go on talking. I can do this myself."

"Did I ruin your evening altogether?" Lainie whined. "Were you about to make dinner or something? Couldn't I offer you—"

"It's quite all right!" I said, the words sounding high pitched, harsh. I was sorry about that, but I just wanted her to come to the point.

I heard him before I saw him.

There was a minor commotion in the kitchen. Then a growl. I wondered fleetingly why I was the only one of the three of us who looked worried about the noise.

Then Bobbin appeared among us and jumped up on the cabinet next to Tony's highball glass.

"I don't understand," I said.

Both Basillio and Lainie looked blankly at me.

"Don't understand what?" she finally asked.

"What Bobbin is doing here—still."

"Bobbin? He lives here."

"Really? Since when?"

"I don't know. Six months. Seven months. Something like that. We hadn't been married very long when Niles got him. He said Bobbin needed a new home and asked me if I liked cats. I said sure. I guess it was Hector who . . . who . . . " Lainie's mouth began to tremble a bit here.

"Lainie, why don't we all sit down?" I suggested.

This poor girl was obviously in tremendous pain over the loss of her husband. Not many of us could handle something like that at age twenty-seven or twenty-eight. And then to be convinced that he'd been murdered. By paté!

I thought about my niece Alison, who had lost her husband, when she was at an even younger age, to suicide. I wondered whether it would be of mutual benefit for Alison and Lainie to get to know each other, in light of what they had in common. But it could just as well turn out to be an opportunity to wallow in the unhappy past.

"When you feel you can, Lainie, why don't you go on?" I said, trying to be kind. I felt very uncomfortable.

"Thanks, Alice. Thanks. I'm okay now. Really. It's just—well, I cannot believe that Niles died accidentally. The cause of his death is named Hector Naciemento."

Tony looked at me, worried. He shook his head quickly, as if to say, *She really is demented.*

"But from what I understand, Lainie, Hector and Niles were old friends. Why would Hector want to do such a thing?"

"I don't know. I really don't know. But that doesn't make it untrue, does it?"

"No."

"I just know that the last few months they weren't getting along well at all. Something about his friendship with Niles changed. It got really poisonous. They were constantly arguing. But I don't know what about. I just know there've been a lot of closed doors around here, and meeting Hector downstairs or in the bar on the corner. And angry whispers on the telephone. I just didn't get it. I tried pressing Niles to tell me what was going on, but he wouldn't. When I downright nagged him about it, he nearly took my head off.

"Niles and Hector had been tight for a

long time, at least as far as I knew. They were even in business together for a while. In the eighties. They owned a restaurant-bar. You know, before the recession. When they had all those stripped-down galleries in the East Village and everyone was making money hand over fist.

"I've only known Niles a year. We married almost immediately after we met. He was basically a really cool older man whose edges just needed smoothing. And I was basically in need of being saved from becoming another Valley girl with a fine arts degree."

Lainie relaxed enough to laugh at her own line then.

"I'm sure you both succeeded," I told her. There was something about this young woman that I was beginning to like. Maybe it was that she seemed to yearn to tell all . . . to tell the truth.

"Thanks," she said, wiping at a tear. "I think Niles really loved me. I loved him, too. And that's why I called on you. Because I heard from Penny Motion, who heard it from somebody—Sam Collins or somebody—that you're a sort of detective."

"That's more or less true."

"I want you to find out what happened. If Hector killed Niles, I want you to prove it. Nail him."

"I don't think so, Lainie."

"Why not?"

"It would be awkward, I think. Grace Ann

is an old friend—an old acquaintance at any rate—and it's clear she's very involved with Hector. And I'm working for Grace Ann and Samantha, so to speak. Even if it's as a mannequin and not a detective. The ethics would get slippery.

"In addition to that, there doesn't seem to be much of a case here. I know you don't want to hear that, but it's what I think. Well, I mean, there's either no case or there are five or six cases. I mean any one of us— if any one of us is crazy enough to do that sort of thing—might have slipped the almond paste into the Cuisinart. I don't think it would have been any easier or harder for Hector to do it than for anyone else who was there.

"*Plus*, there's something about this whole situation that . . . that's . . . I just can't explain. Let's just say that *something* is wrong. Even if it's only me."

Lainie moved very close to me then. Her eyes were like Pancho's—furtive.

"Listen, Alice, Niles and I had nothing in the bank. Nothing. If he hadn't bought the loft outright, I'd have to move out tomorrow. But he did have an insurance policy. And I can borrow some money from my father. Do you understand what I'm saying? I can pay you a good fee."

"No, Lainie."

"Then what do you want?" she screamed

at me. "A pound of flesh? He was murdered, Alice!"

"All right, Lainie! Calm down," I said.

She buried her face in her hands.

I looked at Tony. He turned away. Sisterhood is powerful, I thought grimly.

"I'll make some inquiries for you," I said simply.

"Oh, would you? Would you? I'd be so—"

"Just try not to ride me about this. All right, Lainie? You let me do this in my own way. And try to stay a little bit calmer. And most of all, don't go spreading around that you think Hector Naciemento killed Niles."

Lainie hugged us good-bye, her grip desperate. "I don't mean to cause any trouble. I just want to do the right thing. Because I think Niles really loved—"

"Yes, dear. I think he really did, too," I said.

"Swede, this is nothing but bad news, Swede," Basillio said as we rode down again in that damned elevator.

Out on the street again, I felt the cool fall breeze on my back, in my hair, on my legs. It was heaven.

But it didn't make me feel much like going home and getting into bed with Tony.

I wanted a pizza.

# Chapter 4

I slept late that morning and didn't have time to get any breakfast.

Detective Joseph Stark's blueberry scone, still warm from the oven, looked delicious sitting there on its little bed of tinfoil. I tried not to stare at it. A little rivulet of butter was seeping out from between the two halves of the pastry and heading for his desk blotter.

The detective assigned to the Niles Wiegel death had told me that the only time he could see me was at eight A.M., sharp. So, when I looked over at the clock that morning and discovered it was already seven-thirty, I jumped out of bed, threw dry food into the cats' bowls, and pulled into my clothes without so much as washing my face.

I looked awful and there was a film of gunk on my teeth. No one—but no one—would believe I was the newest sensation in the fashion world.

Detective Stark was very good looking,

and, of course, impeccably groomed. Blond hair and freezing-lake blue eyes. He rose from his chair when I entered the room. He wore a dark jacket, quietly expensive and tailored in that deliberately baggy French–Japanese way, and a heathery sweater very much like the one Niles wore on the day he died.

And he obviously wasn't a hard-bitten police hack or an insensitive boob. He was courteous and attentive while I stated my business and outlined the part I had played in events before and after Niles's death.

It turned out, however, that he didn't quite share my view of the case—or rather, Lainie Wiegel's view.

As it happened, Detective Stark was firmly on Grace Ann's side of the fence. While it was true that the books had not yet been closed, he said, at present the department had no plan to treat Niles's death as anything other than an unfortunate accident. No murder investigation was being considered.

"So you're a private detective," he said pleasantly, taking the first hearty bite of his scone.

"Well, yes and no. I'm not licensed. But I look into things for people . . . friends, usually. And I've worked several times with the New York police. Even as a paid consultant once or twice."

"No kidding? What are you—a psychic? Something like that?"

"No."

"Psychologist?"

"No, I—actually I'm an actress."

He nodded and took a few sips of his steaming coffee. Cappuccino, it appeared to be. Lord, I was hungry.

"So let's see if I have this right," he said, still cordial. "You're a fashion model-actress-unlicensed detective, and this guy Wiegel's widow has retained you to prove one of his best friends killed him at an afternoon party he was throwing for this English dress designer."

He had a few of the facts mixed up, but even so, his deadpan summation of the case was close enough to the reality to make it all sound, to quote Grace Ann, utterly ridiculous. Close enough to justify the official view of Niles's death as an absurd accident.

I had to do something fast, restore a little dignity and credibility to my presentation before Stark wrote me off as an idiot.

"Listen, Detective," I said, "I realize the facts here are a little out of the ordinary. But this isn't a joke to Mrs. Wiegel. She's lost her husband and is convinced that one of his associates caused the death. As I told you, I do have some credentials in criminal investigation—including homicides—and I'm not ready to automatically dismiss the possibility that Niles Wiegel was murdered. So why should you?"

"I'll try to explain a few of the reasons why, Mrs. Nestleton. First of all—"

"Miss. It's Miss Nestleton."

"Oh. I see." He paused there.

Damn him. Stark was a couple of years younger than I. How dare he treat me as if I were a dotty old maid!

"First of all, what, Detective?"

"First of all, I think the facts here are more than a *little* bit out of the ordinary.

"Secondly, it's going to be pretty rough showing that anybody in Wiegel's crowd knew about his problem with almonds. I mean, how would you prove something like that? In fact, about the only person who'd be pretty much sure to know that would be the widow herself—right?

"And then, even if someone else did do it, went in there and dumped almonds in the sandwich spread, who's to say they did it with the intention of killing the man? Maybe they just thought it would add a nice touch. I mean, you've got to admit it's not exactly a surefire way of killing somebody. How do you know how much to put in? How do you know he doesn't have some medicine he can swallow to reverse the effects of the almonds?"

I had to admit, those were very good questions. I didn't have the answers to them.

"You've raised exactly the kind of questions I was hoping the police would follow up on," I told him. "And a few more. Like motive and opportunity and means. You know, Sergeant Stark, the basics of investigation."

"Oh yes, the old basics. You *are* a detective, aren't you?"

He had an indulgent smile on his perfect lips, along with a couple of crumbs. I wanted to smack them all off with one blow.

"I guess you aren't convinced yet, are you?" he asked. And then he checked his watch conspicuously.

"No. Not really."

"I'm sorry about that. I wish I had more time to go over the case with you, share my notes and stuff. But, unfortunately . . . ." He looked at the watch again and shook his head as if not being able to spend more time with me was the major regret of his life.

"Well, anyway," he said, "it would be an interesting case for Miss Marple, wouldn't it?"

I wasn't sure I had heard him correctly. "Excuse me?"

"Miss Marple. My lady friend reads a lot of Agatha Christie books. She says it helps her relax."

"Oh really? What does your ladylove do, Detective?"

"She's a curator at the Museum of Modern Art."

"Well . . . my goodness. That would explain it."

"Yes. I think I'll tell her about your friends. Maybe she'll recognize the plot. It sounds a whole lot like one she was reading the other night: *Poison in the Paté.*" He smiled broadly as he picked up his coffee cup again.

That did it.

"Detective Stark, I want to thank you for your time," I said acidly. "I'll be sure to report how nice you were to me if your superiors ever become involved in this case."

I got up and headed for the door.

"Oh, hold on. Just a moment, Miss Nestleton."

I looked back at him.

"Here," he said, proffering a small white square. "Take my card. Life is so strange that . . . Who knows? You might turn up something after all. I'm sure it would be a pleasure to work with you. Even on a case as . . . uh, nutty as this one."

As I passed through the door to his office, I heard a click. Detective Stark had picked up the receiver of his telephone.

Was he eager to share this one with the guys or was he calling to verify my claim of having worked with the department in the past?

I left the station house as fast as my legs could carry me. On the street there was the pervasive smell of horse manure. Attached to the precinct house were the stables for the mounted police horses. From deep inside came a whinnying chorus that sounded strangely like laughter.

Damn, damn, damn! I was no more convinced than the police that Niles Wiegel had been murdered. But I wasn't going to be laughed at by an arrogant little bureaucrat like Stark. I didn't care how blue his eyes were. If he was an example of the new breed of cop, I preferred the chain-smoking stereotype with big feet and bad toupees.

I *was* going to investigate Niles's death. I guess I had my new job, my new commitment. For real.

Up the quiet block—all the painters and performance artists still sleeping in their loft beds—I walked right past the new black and white-tiled cafe whose name had been imprinted on Detective Stark's coffee container.

At Grand Street I turned into an old diner on wheels and ordered the special breakfast, which came with hot buttered hominy grits.

# Chapter 5

I took a long shower and read the paper and picked up around the apartment and groomed the cats—all the things there had been no time to do earlier in the morning.

I was still angry at Stark, convinced that if I'd been twenty-five years old, or anything but an actress—or simply a man—he'd never have treated me in that infuriating way. It galled me all the more that he was articulate and sharp rather than a dummy. That just made his behavior all the more inexcusable.

I planned to go over to Boutique Ariel, to talk to the Collins sisters, but I knew the shop wouldn't be open for at least another hour and a half.

The stores in the Village had even later hours. On many mornings I was eager to get my errands out of the way or go shopping for things for the loft, but I wound up killing time until one in the afternoon, when the antique store or the bath shop or the bookstore opened its doors. It made you wonder whether the owners were independently wealthy, running their businesses more for amusement than income. Of course, when I was broke, they could have opened between one and three in the morning for all I cared.

I called Tony about ten o'clock to tell him of my misadventure with Stark, but he didn't answer. It was unusual for him to be out and about so early unless he had spent the night here. One of the many holdovers from my farm upbringing is that I am still an early riser. And when I get up, Tony gets up. Or else the cats go for him.

I made coffee and drank it while I wrote down a list of all those present the day of the shoot. I already knew where most of the—was it time to start calling them suspects?—lived. Tony and Alison I eliminated from the list immediately. I'd have to find addresses for Penny Motion; Sidney Rickover, the attorney; and Hector, although he might actually be living with Grace Ann.

I tried to dress with a little panache, deciding to add the lovely scarf that Grace Ann had given me to my short wool dress. And I searched until I located the plain diamond-stud earrings that my ex-husband had given me as a wedding present. I even bypassed my trusty brown boots and chose instead some moderate heels.

Bushy sat on the old art deco vanity I'd bought at the flea market and revarnished. He watched me make up and change my hair from ponytail to french roll and back down again.

At last I was ready. I put on my big gray sweater, the one with the oversize black buttons, and left the apartment—feeling rather pretty, to be honest.

Tony had asked me the other day why I didn't make more jokes. I wondered fleetingly if he thought I didn't make enough effort with my appearance. God, I must be getting old, I thought. The day that I start worrying about Basillio is the day I know I've turned a corner in life. But what corner?

Would I now become obsessed with my looks? With my fading attractiveness? Would I start taking Grace Ann and Samantha's world seriously?

It was almost enough to make me turn around, go home and change into jeans.

But I didn't.

I walked the twenty-odd blocks into Chelsea. My own neighborhood was awake, hopping now. The cafes were spilling over with the breakfast-at-eleven-thirty set. The dog walkers were out in full force. Muffled jukebox music leaked out of the bars where the prenoon drinkers congregated for the day's first shot of courage.

The boutique was down a wide flight of stairs with a railing painted and repainted until it shone like black lacquer. On the sidewalk a large, hand-painted sign in Art

Nouveau lettering announced ARIEL/LADIES BOUTIQUE. Samantha and Grace Ann lived in the brownstone above the shop.

The sisters had always managed to make the most of what were decidedly modest quarters. There wasn't a lot to the boutique, but it was an extremely pretty place—hand-turned creations done in luxurious fabrics displayed here and there like artwork; wrought-iron and glass cases rescued from long forgotten emporiums; knickknacks lovingly collected from sources as disparate as junked ocean liners and rural New Jersey yard sales.

There was no sign of either Collins sister in the store.

I had never met Julia before, the girl behind the sales desk, but she was effusive in her greeting to me. Perhaps that was because she recognized the scarf immediately. I made sure to compliment her on her handiwork.

We chatted pleasantly for a couple of minutes after I told her I was one of the models in the new ad campaign. Much to my surprise, she had met Alison, who'd come in just yesterday to pick out a few things. Trying to head off another discussion about my niece's bone structure, I asked Julia if she thought the Collins sisters could speak to me for a few minutes.

"Grace Ann and Sam are both out," she told me. "I don't expect them back anytime soon. Is there something I could help you with?"

"Maybe you can."

I didn't exactly know how to go on from there. I needed to pry a little, needed to know some pretty personal information about the sisters and Hector. But I didn't want to compromise Julia or make her think I was pressing her for dirt about her employers. Even if I was.

"If Grace Ann and Samantha are both away, I wonder if Hector is around," I said.

Julia smiled. "Hector? No. He doesn't come in to the shop very much."

"Oh. I thought I might find him 'in.'" And I pointed vaguely heavenward, meaning the flat above.

"I don't think so. I haven't heard anything up there for hours."

Well, that didn't tell me anything one way or the other about where Hector was living. I decided to try a different tack.

"Grace Ann must be getting careless," I said playfully. "God knows, if Hector were mine I'd know where he is at every moment of the day."

"Tell me about it," Julia said, nodding in agreement. "Isn't he gorgeous?"

"Well. Grace Ann deserves to be happy. She's so beautiful. And so talented. But then, they both are, aren't they?"

"Oh yes! Samantha's a genius. I'm going to school now, but I know if I live a thousand years I'll never be able to cut the way she does. It's just magic."

"It's a pity Samantha doesn't have someone like Hector, too," I said distractedly, pretending to be fascinated by a pair of hammered tin earrings. "There just don't seem to be enough fabulous men to go around."

"Sam could have any man she wanted," Julia said, sounding as if she felt Samantha needed defending. "She's just one of those women who doesn't seem to have any interest in that."

It was time to lie like a thief. The young woman was primed. A good investigation is never, ever, an ethical endeavor.

"Isn't that strange?" I said. "You know, I've always believed the same thing. My brother Edwin was terribly in love with her in the old days, when she and Grace Ann first came north. She never paid him the least attention. But of course that was way before your time."

"You've known them that long?"

"Ages and ages."

"Things haven't changed much then," the girl said, laughing. "Sidney's gaga about her. And she treats him like—well, like her attorney. Which is what he is. But he'd like to be a lot more than that, as I'm sure you know. I feel kind of sorry for him, even if he is dripping money."

So. No definitive answer about Hector's living arrangements, but I'd gotten another piece of information. For whatever it was worth. Actually, it was more confirmation than news. Sidney Rickover had certainly appeared to be mooning over Samantha at the shoot that day.

Not that Rickover was any match for Hector Naciemento in the beauty department, but I did wonder why Samantha was so completely indifferent to the lawyer's devotion. He was a nice enough looking man, and wealthy, according to Julia.

Was Samantha the only fifty-year-old virgin in New York? Was she, as Julia had put it, simply not interested in *that*? Was she holding out for another Hector? Or maybe the same Hector—the one who already belonged to her sister?

Just as Julia began to explain to me why black was out for evening wear this upcoming season, the strains of a Bach partita wafted down from the ceiling. It was no record. And not a radio from the sidewalk above. The music was live. I remembered that Samantha Collins played the harpsichord.

Julia flushed, stopping midsentence.

She had obviously been told to say that the Collins sisters were not at home to anyone.

"Oh, how lucky," I said quickly, giving her a way out. "Samantha's come back early. Would you be good enough to ask if she could spare just a few minutes?"

With no other choice, Julia went up the stairs at the back of the shop and complied with my request.

I won't say that Samantha Collins was rude to me when I walked into the parlor where she sat at the massive harpsichord like a starved Titian cherub. I suppose it was simply that she had nothing like her sister's skills for pretense and social lying, finely honed by a lifetime of denying the obvious and suffering the inane.

"Hello, Samantha. I know you must be busy. I won't visit long."

"Alice," was all she said.

"Samantha, I just wanted to say I feel terrible for you and Grace Ann. Not just for the problems with the business and Fliss Francis and all that. I mean I'm sorry about your friend Niles."

"Yes," she said dully. "That's what's important, isn't it?"

"I understood from Grace Ann that you weren't feeling quite up to par. It's nice to see you getting back to—"

She interrupted with what was almost a snort. "Getting back to work. Getting back to business. Oh my, yes. My sister has almost got me back on my feet again. If you've come to see her, as just about everyone does, she's over at the loft now."

"Loft?"

"I mean the plant. The factory." She virtually spat out the word *factory*. "Imagine that. A factory! It's what we've become, darling. Turning out mass-produced garments—for the masses. Makes sense, doesn't it?" She seemed to be laughing. I didn't know for sure.

Samantha then gestured at the overstuffed chair and I quickly took a seat.

"You're a little behind the times, it sounds like. Didn't anyone tell you about our Forsyth Street sweat mill?" she said.

Oh, yes. I'd forgotten. I *had* been told at the shoot that with the Collins sisters' new success, the bulk of the actual sewing work had been moved from the back of the downstairs shop to new quarters on the edge of Chinatown. Instead of Samantha and one other hired seamstress, there was now a select staff of experienced illustrators and seamstresses.

Even so, I was sure that Samantha's characterization of their output as mass production was mostly exaggeration. They were simply doing more than one-of-a-kind garments now, to be sold in some of the most exclusive shops in the city.

"You know, Samantha, my business hasn't exactly been wonderful lately either," I said. "I mean the cat-sitting. And I really miss taking care of Bobbin."

At the mention of Bobbin, she looked over at me, and stiffened visibly, but she said not a word.

There was something oddly familiar in

Samantha's tension-filled posture and the expanding variety of weird expressions appearing and then disappearing from her face.

I made yet another fond comment about Bobbin the cat. But it evoked nothing but more disturbing facial contortions from her.

I then made a fatal mistake.

"Hector seems like a very nice man," I said. "Is Grace Ann serious about him?"

Her slender hands knotted into fists and with one of them she swept her sheet music onto the floor. "Please leave me now, Alice."

I bounded out of the chair and walked swiftly to the front door, too stunned to say good-bye.

I wasn't hungry, but I poured a huge glass of wine for myself when I set the ham sandwich down in front of Tony.

I was trying to put together a comprehensible, blow-by-blow narration of the whole terrible day for him.

"What happened to the cheese?" he complained. "Where are the pickles?"

"For god sakes, Basillio, get it yourself."

"So what do you think you'll do now?" he asked, his head in the refrigerator. "I mean after we track that cop down and break his feet."

"I wish."

It made me sick to think I might really

have to go to Stark again if I did turn up some evidence.

Tony walked back to the table, or rather he sauntered with that kind of street bop New York men seem to cultivate. His walk made me think of something truly horrible. What if it wasn't a murder? Or even a traditional accident. What if it was one of those "lah di da" kind of deaths? What if someone went to get a glass of water, passed the almond paste, and, without thinking, scooped some out and flung it into the paté? Just on impulse. Maybe a spoon was lying there. Just on bloody impulse.

Oh, this wasn't good! To think like this. Get it out of your mind, I said to myself. Then I remembered that it was precisely this scenario that Detective Stark had offered up.

"I've got to find out what the hell's going on with Samantha Collins," I said. "But maybe I'll have to go in through the back door, so to speak. Through Grace Ann. Meanwhile, I suppose I'll target Hector. And that girl, Penny. I'll need your help with a little surveillance, Tony."

He was chewing his sandwich, not answering.

"Well, can you help?"

"I guess so, Swede. If I'm not too busy."

"Busy with what? The racetrack?"

"No. Just . . . work. Sketches I'm trying to

work up for that theater on Sullivan Street. I mean, I'll help you out if I can."

"Well, thank you so much, Tony."

"Okay, okay. I'm yours."

Samantha's behavior haunted me all day, even during the early evening movie that Basillio and I went to, and walked out of after forty minutes.

We had espresso in one of the new coffee places that keep popping up like mushrooms in the urban forest. It was all I could do not to grab a spoon and hijack the last of Basillio's chocolate-on-chocolate ice cream indulgence. But I was still under the Collins sisters' no-sweets fiat until the fashion shoot was over and done.

Tony laughed at me through his whipped cream.

Who *didn't* I want to slug today?

Once we were back at my place, I made up my mind to call Grace Ann and at least find out why Bobbin, the beloved family pet, had been given to the Wiegels. I couldn't see how a simple question like that would tax the venerable southern flower.

Thankfully, it was Grace Ann who picked up the phone. I identified myself and tried in my stumbling way to apologize for any distress I had caused poor Sam, as her associates called her.

She assured me in honeyed verse that all would be well and I wasn't to worry about what had happened. Samantha just needed to get back to her work.

And then, when in the most casual way imaginable I inquired about Bobbin's home with Niles and Lainie, she hung up in my face.

I wanted to scream.

Just before I fell asleep that night, I realized what memory Samantha Collins was bringing back into focus with her frozen limbs and twisting face. She looked like Mrs. Bean, the crazy woman who sat on her porch swing each night in the little Minnesota farming town where I grew up.

# Chapter 6

Tony and I met at a Latino coffee bar on 8th Avenue. They served the best café con leche I had ever had in my life.

Another selling point of the place was that it opened early, at seven A.M.

And best of all, we could see the Collins brownstone from the coffee shop counter.

All we could do for the moment was drink coffee and wait. The empty streets were hushed and deserted in the early autumn light. The dance theater and aerobics studio across the avenue was shut. The trendy French bistro next to it would not open its doors for hours. Even the boom boxes that usually rang out salsa music and rap from the fire escapes of the last of the old tenements had gone silent.

Basillio ordered a fantastic-looking pastry shaped like a squashed chef's hat. It was covered with glazed apricots. After he'd eaten that, he started in on a flan that the waiter was just about to place on the display cake stand. The warm custard and sugary dark caramel on his plate came up at me in waves.

"So what are you doing?" Tony asked making fun of me again. "Studying to become an anorexic or something?"

"Watching my weight, you insensitive clod. I made a pact with the Collinses when I agreed to do this stupid modeling thing, and I'm going to keep it. Don't you know the camera adds pounds to your appearance?"

"Dames," he said in mock exasperation, doing a bad *Guys and Dolls* accent. Then he leaned over on his counter stool and kissed me on the nose.

That was a singularly un-Tony like thing to have done. I looked at him for a long moment, stunned, before returning my gaze to the building up 15th Street.

"Swede, I think we just lucked out."

Yes. Tony was right.

It was 8:30. Walking out of the Collins front door and making his way lightly down the steps was Hector Naciemento.

A minute later, we waved good-bye to the counterman and set out after Hector, who had turned onto 8th and begun to walk downtown.

When he crossed 14th Street and made the turn onto Greenwich Avenue, so did we, except that he was on the south side of the avenue and we were on the north. Or was it, respectively, west and east? Greenwich, like the Village as a whole, seemed to twist this way and that with every block. It's hard to keep one's bearings without a compass.

Hector was dressed in gray gabardine trousers, white polo shirt, and a pebbly textured gray cardigan with subtle red stripes. He carried a small leather duffel. It was quite a pace that he set. Tony and I continued to follow him discreetly, but keeping up with his brisk, steady gait wasn't so easy. We walked in almost total silence, not merely because we were afraid he might hear us and look over, but because we were meting out our breath.

Hector continued on Greenwich until he hit 7th Avenue. There he continued south.

On he walked—past the famous Village Vanguard, past the new pizzeria and the age-old hamburger joint. Soon he was at Christopher Street, where the Village Cigar Store, which had changed hands more times than even the most devoted local historian could count, still traded in Coronas and lottery tickets, cheap watches and chewing gum.

We were in my own neighborhood now, only two blocks east of my place. But Hector went on, now on the fringe of the Village and heading into TriBeCa.

The avenue widened, then narrowed again—making Basillio and me nervous that Hector might take note of us—then widened once more. We left Houston Street behind. And crowded, crazy Canal Street, car horns blaring, exhaust fumes gushing from the entrance to the Holland Tunnel.

At last! When Hector reached Chambers Street, he stopped in front of a squat little building, quite new, with a brightly colored flag flapping on its pole from a second story window. It announced the High End Athletic Club.

While our subject had his workout, steam, and massage—presumably—Tony and I sat in the little makeshift park across from the gym, drinking sodas we bought from the hot dog vendor.

"This guy's in pretty good shape," Tony said grudgingly as he finished his Pepsi. "What does he need a gym for, anyway?"

"Young people go to gyms today as a matter of course. Hector's still a young man, Tony. No more than thirty-one or -two," I replied, a bit amused at the undercurrent of jealousy in his voice. My club soda wasn't very cold, but I drank it straight down just the same. I was thirsty after that forced march.

When the subject emerged from the building, two hours later, he looked unabashedly invigorated and beautiful, fairly bursting with good health, damp black hair slicked away from his forehead. His step, if anything, was even livelier.

The next leg of Hector's hike pulled us, a half block behind him all the way, several blocks north of the gym, into SoHo.

On Broome Street, Hector walked into a nondescript storefront in the middle of the block. When it was safe, I walked by the store hurriedly, head averted slightly, and discovered that it was the premises of an old Italian tailor. Then I joined Tony in the doorway of a carpeting store across the street. Hector remained inside for about forty minutes.

The next stop was a roomy and quiet trattoria on Spring Street. Hector was hungry. So were we. Hector was shown to a corner table where a place for one had already been set. We took up places at the counter of the pizza parlor across from the restaurant. Basillio had two slices. I ate a dead green salad and cadged an anchovy from Tony's paper plate.

"Maybe he'll get hit by a bike messenger," Tony speculated, a bit weary.

Near Washington Square, Hector got a shoe shine. At a cigarette store on 11th Street, he bought an Italian men's fashion magazine and a disposable lighter. He stopped by Balducci's and emerged ten minutes later carrying a pastry box. He tried on a pair of shoes at a new place farther up 6th Avenue.

"What a boring life this guy has," Tony observed while we stood in a bus shelter across from the shoe store. "I always figured gigolos were kind of glamorous."

"We don't know he's a gigolo," I pointed out. "Perhaps he's independently wealthy."

"Then what's he doing with a woman old enough to be his mother?"

"You're a little behind the times, aren't you, Tony? Grace Ann is a lovely, ambitious, sophisticated woman. Maybe Hector's with her because of all those things."

"And maybe he's with her because right now she's making big bucks and knows a lot of New York celebrities."

"Maybe. But even if that's true, it's not out of the question that he could also have feelings for her. Let's not be so quick to judge," I replied, knowing it was very bad to trivialize a suspect. Bad people love also.

Hector really surprised us after that. He got into a cab.

We had to make a run for it and locate another one before his got away from us.

"Let me do this, Swede," Basillio said excitedly, leaning forward toward the driver. "How many times in a guy's life does he get to say 'Follow that cab'?"

And that was exactly how he put it to the bored cabby.

We tailed Hector all the way up to Columbus Avenue.

When Hector got out of his taxi, he walked directly into a cafe with tables on a glass-enclosed patio. Basillio and I sought cover at the rival coffee bar across the avenue.

We needn't have bothered. Hector wouldn't have taken any notice of us even if we'd followed him inside. As soon as he walked into the cafe a young woman in towering high heel boots and a tight, puce-colored skirt no longer than her black leather motorcycle jacket—at buttocks level, that is—got to her feet and raced over to him. They began to kiss like lovers reunited after World War II.

"Well, Tony, looks like the plot has thickened. Or should I say curdled? Look at who he's kissing."

Basillio was looking, looking hard.

"Can't you see who it is?" I said. "It's the girl from the Wiegels' loft. The makeup and lighting girl. Penny."

"Right. Penny Motion."

Penny and Hector raced two blocks up Columbus and entered an apartment building at the corner of 76th Street.

An hour passed. Tony and I agreed that there seemed little point to waiting for Hector to come out of that building any time soon. After all, he'd even thought to bring dessert.

I called Lainie Wiegel that evening from the Japanese restaurant where Tony and I were having dinner. I told her not to expect a lot of help from the police, based on my meeting with Stark.

I didn't tell her what Tony and I had seen

earlier in the day, but I did say there had been enough developments to make me remain on the investigation for a while longer.

Back at the table, Basillio was drinking sake as if there were no tomorrow. I let go of my dieting resolve and asked the waitress to bring me one of those demure little cups as well.

It had been a tiring day. But I felt good. I couldn't look forward to a big fat fee—no more than the expense money Lainie had insisted on paying—but I seemed to be getting more and more wrapped in this strange investigation. At least one cat was out of the bag now.

I had an appointment with Sidney Rickover for the following afternoon.

"I guess you feel justified in your low opinion of Hector now," I told Basillio. "Well, it looks like you were right."

"Score one for me," Tony said, holding up the empty bottle as a signal to the waitress. She was back with a refill in seconds.

"We'll try to do a little more surveillance on Hector tomorrow, but I've got something else to do in the afternoon. Then I think it might be a good idea to put you on Penny. You can handle that alone, can't you? We know where she lives."

"Who?"

"Penny, I said. I think we'll do Hector for one more day and then I want you to get on Penny. Can you?"

Tony's expression startled me. He was actually snarling. "Do you ever think, Swede, that this hobby of yours is kind of seedy?"

I felt as though he had slapped me. But I tried to keep an even tone in my voice. "What did you say?"

"I mean, how does it feel to go around spying on people, invading people's privacy all the time?"

"Excuse me, Tony, but I don't 'spy' on people. At least not in the way you're making it sound—as if I do it for fun. Or blackmail. Or because I'm a snoop. But if I have to do it in the course of catching a murderer who might go free otherwise, then . . . then I'll spy. Privacy doesn't seem so important when you compare it to murder, does it?"

Tony poured more sake into our cups.

"Well, I don't like it. No matter what you call it or why you do it," he said petulantly. "It's nasty."

"I don't think anyone has ever called me nasty before. Certainly not someone I consider my friend. And certainly not to my face."

"I didn't say *you* were nasty. I said the work was. And dumb. And dangerous. And a waste of energy. You're supposed to be an actress, not a keyhole voyeur. It's not the work you were put on earth to do."

"Fine. Then don't help me."

"Take it easy! I didn't say I wasn't going to help you."

"Perhaps you shouldn't if it offends your sense of ethics, Tony . . . if you think it isn't *fair*. But of course I have to wonder if you're just in a bad mood because you're jealous of Hector Naciemento."

"I am not jealous of that peacock with a tan. I'm just—"

"Just what, Tony?"

"Just . . . I don't know."

*"What?"*

"Ah, forget it. It's nothing."

"Yes it is. It obviously is."

"No! Let's just drop it, okay?"

I didn't answer.

Tony's manner changed then, and he broke into a crooked smile. "As a matter of fact," he said teasingly, "I'll tell you the only thing that I'm worried about right now. I'm worried you don't get enough to eat. And here comes your sukiyaki right now."

The waitress set the tray down on our table and uncovered the heavy pot. I was so transported by the heady brown broth and the blinding white of the rice that I put my anger and concern over Basillio's flareup aside for the night.

Something was really troubling Tony. It might have been another one of his tempests in a teapot. Or perhaps it was quite serious. Was he ill? Was he broke? How was I to know? He was shutting me out.

I'd get it out of him one way or another, though. Sooner or later.

Then I realized that I probably didn't want to know, because it probably had something to do with his ex-wife, or visitation rights with his kids, or with child support.

Suddenly Tony leaned over the table and in an ugly whisper said: "You really want to know why I'm mad, Swede? You really want to know? I'll tell you. Because never once did you ask me what I think about this case. Not once!"

He sat back.

"Okay, Tony. Tell me what you think."

"Lainie killed her husband."

For a moment I was too startled to say anything. Then I asked simply: "Why?"

"Motive one: she couldn't stand to eat any more of his goddamn paté. Motive two: she wanted the loft all to herself so she could start her own rap group—called Bobbin and the SoHo Rats."

"You're either drunk or crazy," I noted with a smile.

"Well, Swede . . . from the mouths of crazy, drunken babes often comes wisdom."

The rice was delicious.

# Chapter 7

The phone rang while I was putting on my makeup. I was due in Sidney Rickover's office in a couple of hours.

It was Sidney's executive secretary. Mr. Rickover was terribly sorry, but he'd been called away to Denver on business and would not be able to keep our appointment. He would phone me in a day or two, as soon as he returned, and reschedule our meeting. Was that all right?

It would have to be all right, wouldn't it? What choice did I have?

One more thing, the secretary said, just for her records, "It's the Blankman merger, isn't it, that you're going to be discussing with Sidney?"

No, it's the pussycat mystery, I wanted to answer. But I managed not to say anything more than "Not really."

I was annoyed, naturally, that my appointment with Sidney Rickover was being canceled. But perhaps it was for the best. I wasn't exactly razor sharp that morning. In fact, I was tired and irritable. I hadn't had the best night's sleep.

It was while I was brushing Bushy, and at the same time attempting to wrest my panty hose from Pancho's clutches, that the phone rang again.

Julia, the girl from Boutique Ariel, was on the other end of the line. She was effusively friendly, but behind that I could sense some nervousness. After a few minutes of small talk, she came to the point: Grace Ann and Samantha had managed to reschedule with Fliss Francis and they wanted to resume the fashion shoot on the next day. They realized what short notice it was, but could I be ready at ten in the morning?

I hesitated for just a second, thinking that the Collins sisters were two of the strangest ladies I had ever met in my life. One day they're unceremoniously kicking you out of the door—or hanging up on you without explanation—and the next day it's business as usual, as if nothing had happened. They seemed to be able to turn that legendary southern graciousness on and off like a light switch.

Maybe, I thought, to make it big in the rag trade, you had to stop and turn on a dime. And turn again. And stop again. Like a clock with a berserk mainspring.

But I agreed to the photography session, anyway. My investigation of the Collinses' circle of friends was just getting started.

And I didn't know how else I was going to reestablish contact with the two sisters. Besides, Pancho and Bushy needed *boneless* sardines, and I needed winter boots made in Finland.

"Okay," I said. "I'll be ready."

"Oh, that's fabulous, Alice. And now, there's one other favor you could do us."

"What?"

She paused. I could almost hear her counting beats, like an acting student . . . like the three-beat pause before a revelation or a confession.

"We were wondering if we could shoot at your place."

"*My* place?"

"Yes. Grace Ann said your loft would be the perfect place for the shoot—windows, brick, light, space, everything. And you wouldn't have to fuss or clean up or anything. Fliss wants the place to look like you just woke up in the morning, he said. You know—kind of—oh, what's that word? Tousled . . . .Alice . . . are you still there?"

"Yes, I'm here. By the way, Julia, where are Grace Ann and Samantha? I would have expected one of them to be making this call."

"Oh, they're at Forsyth Street. They're flying around here and there, you know. There's a ton of work to do."

"I see."

"So what do you think, Alice? I mean,

there would just be you and Alison, Sarah and Eugenie Putnam—they're mother and daughter jewelry makers who're modeling the pajamas—Grace Ann and Sam, Hector, Penny, and Fliss, and maybe a couple of extra assistants. That's all. Would it be too much to ask?"

That's all—a mere ten or twelve people in my apartment first thing in the morning. Astonishing! I had to laugh. Whose assistant was going to call me next? Bobbin's? And what kind of request was she going to make?

"All right, Julia. Tell them it's okay. But I don't know about my niece. She may be busy."

"No problem," Julia said. "She's available."

So. Alison had become best buddies with the Collinses. Perhaps the time would come when I'd have to ask her to act as intermediary with them. We'd see how long it took before they were giving *her* the cold shoulder. That wasn't very likely, though, as it was my guess that Alison was dropping vast quantities of Felix's money at Boutique Ariel.

What a nasty thing to think about my niece, I realized. There was no evidence that she was squandering Felix's money.

And, if she was, what did it matter? Felix Drinnan, the fiftyish psychiatrist with whom she now lived, had more money than Rocke-feller.

And he was the most kindly and generous man I knew. He had given me a wonderful loft to live in, rent free.

Maybe I still resented the fact that Alison had moved out of my apartment to live with a man twice her age who looked like the old movie actor Brian Donlevy, right down to the mustache.

In fact, other than his mustache, Felix had no vices. Unless collecting was a vice. He was invariably bubbling over one of his collecting manias—from rare stamps to coins to fountain pens to Haitian art.

Still, I had this very strong intuition that Alison had quietly become one of Boutique Ariel's better customers.

Intuition?

Perhaps that was too strong a word. I decided to keep it in the category of "guess."

Just as it was my guess that the sisters had asked Lainie Wiegel if they could resume shooting in her loft and she'd turned them down. Either that, or it had penetrated, even to the self-absorbed Collinses, that going back to the Wiegel place to do the shoot that ended in Niles's death would be forcing Lainie to relive the nightmare.

I wasn't going to check out these speculations with Lainie, but I did decide to call her. After all, I had the free time now that Sidney had stood me up.

Since I had no trusty assistant, I placed the call myself.

I tied a piece of string to a little cloth catnip mouse and put old Bobbin through his paces all around the living room. We had big fun while Lainie made espresso.

When she joined me on the sofa, I undid the string and tossed the mouse over to the other side of the room, where Bobbin promptly fell asleep with his nose buried in the toy.

"Lainie, I've been going over in my mind the things that happened here that day."

She nodded her understanding of exactly which day I meant, as if to forestall my actually using Niles's name or saying the word "died."

"I have to depend on you and the others who were here for your observations, because most of the time I was behind that screen changing in and out of outfits."

"Yes, I know," she said shakily. "But I might as well have been behind a screen, too. There was so much going on. Everybody coming and going. Who could keep track of who was where?"

Exactly. If indeed someone had murdered Niles, that is what he or she had counted on: our not being able to keep track of who was where.

"Do you remember seeing anyone other than Niles handling the food?"

"No—well, wait. I think at one point Niles sent your friend into the kitchen for something. Yes, I remember seeing him carrying that red lacquered tray we have."

That wasn't very useful. She meant Basillio. I knew that he had not done away with Niles. And I'd already quizzed Tony about what he saw lying around on the kitchen counters.

"Since you suspect Hector so strongly," I said, "can you think of anything he said or did that was suspicious or hostile or threatening?"

"Not really, no. In fact, he and Niles seemed to be making an effort to laugh together and be friendly, like old times. But there was something phony about it. I knew it was some kind of act. I knew they weren't getting along at all."

"Any specific memories of seeing Hector go into the kitchen by himself?"

She thought about it for a minute, almost willing the image of Hector slinking into the kitchen to pop up in her mind, but in the end she shook her head. "I don't know. He may have. He may not have. But I'm fairly sure he would have known about Niles's allergy to almonds. Niles used to joke about it all the time, with everyone."

Suddenly, almost violently, she brought her hands to her mouth. Her eyes became wild and desperate as if she could not bear to speak again about that banal, stupid, murderous paté. The attack or spell, or whatever it was, vanished as quickly as it had come. She signaled with her hands that she was fine.

"Okay. Anyone else in the kitchen alone?" I asked.

"Maybe—maybe Penny. Yes, I think so. But I may be making that up. See, I think I heard her telling Sam Collins that she was on a twenty-four-hour water fast. I guess it's how she keeps her figure. So, I don't actually remember whether I literally saw her go in to the kitchen several times, or whether she just mentioned going to get water several times a day."

"What else do you know about Penny?"

"Not much. I only met her a few times before that day. She hangs out at Perfection, I think."

"Perfection?"

"It's a bar on Mercer Street, where Hector and Niles used to go sometimes. Niles and I stopped in there for drinks once. I think we saw Penny there. But I didn't really know her. She's Hector's friend."

Yes, that much was clear, based on that steamy kiss that Tony and I had witnessed. This was not the time to reveal such things to Lainie, though. Among other reasons for not telling her about Hector and Penny, I didn't want to risk her telling Grace Ann about it—yet.

"Did Niles tell you much about Hector?"

"What do you mean?"

"How they met, for instance. Or where Hector was born. Or how he felt about Grace Ann. That kind of thing."

"Oh. No, we didn't talk about him that much, I guess. I know he's from Brazil, but he's been in the States since he was a child. His family had money once, but now . . . they're dead, both of them, I think. And he wasn't very careful with what they left him.

"As I told you, he and Niles used to run a cafe together, but that was before I knew Niles."

"Did you ever know any of the other women he saw? Before Grace Ann, I mean."

"No."

"Do you know if he takes drugs?"

"Who doesn't?"

"Beg pardon?"

"Everybody does something some time, don't they? Hector doesn't do any more than anyone else."

I took that in. I guess my surprise and confusion had something to do with our generational difference. I didn't think about it much, but I assumed younger people had stopped taking drugs with the end of the disco era.

"Anyway," Lainie went on, "Hector's too devoted to his looks to do much physical damage to himself with drugs. He *is* beautiful, you know."

"Yes," I agreed. "But you know that old saying, Beauty is as beauty does."

"No," she said, "I don't. But I guess I waited too long to be curious about Hector. The last month or so, while he and Niles were quarreling, Niles wouldn't even discuss Hector with me. He acted as if he didn't even want me to mention his name."

The remainder of my visit with Lainie went much the same way. She had only limited knowledge of Niles's friends, because, she said, she and Niles had been together for such a short time.

I wondered about Lainie. I wondered more and more whether Basillio was on to something about her evasiveness. I disagreed, however, with his characterization of her as dumb. I suspected that she was either genuinely in the dark about her late husband's friends, or that she was a great deal shrewder than we were giving her credit for.

Lainie rode downstairs with me, asking for assurances that I would not give up on the investigation. And I gave them to her, if a bit warily.

Together we walked to Prince Street, where she did her marketing. As we parted at the doorway of the butcher shop, I heard the tall, good-looking man behind the counter begin to express his condolences to her. He spoke with a heavy French accent.

Lainie Wiegel—quite the little SoHo widow. Young, pretty, and now, alone. And even if Niles had left her no money, she did own a beautiful loft in one of the poshest neighborhoods in Manhattan.

Wasn't it interesting—in SoHo, even the butchers are attractive.

I phoned Tony from the street. He was out. But I told his machine—or rather, my old machine—about the photo session and that I was expecting him at the loft that night with his surveillance report on Penny Motion.

I bought a small, precooked veal roast at the Bleecker Street butcher shop I had come to know since moving into the neighborhood. The help there was quite a different story from the slim-hipped European émigrés who seemed to have a lock on the food provision industry in SoHo.

In my neighborhood, the butchers were third-generation Italian Americans, portly and balding and invariably sporting a blood-stained apron. They liked flirting with me and I liked letting them.

I picked up fresh fruit from a street vendor and a reasonably priced bottle of red wine from the musty old liquor store on Hudson Street and headed home.

The cats went crazy when they got a whiff of that still-warm veal. They begged piteously. But I was steadfast. I put out more kitty health food for them—it's dry as the veritable bone—and had to walk around the loft with Bushy's accusing eyes burning into my back.

I figured that a nice meal would comfort and relax Tony and that he might get loose enough to tell me what had been troubling him lately. The more I had thought about his behavior in the Japanese restaurant, the more worried I had become.

But when he arrived, he hardly looked in need of mothering. He was jauntily carrying his own bottle of wine under one arm, and he was bursting with excitement.

"So, Miss Nestleton also known as Twiggy, maybe you're going to be in every slick magazine in town. But I'm the one making the bold moves in your investigation," Tony said in triumph.

"What bold moves? What do you mean, Tony?"

"I mean I've outsnooped the snoop. Outspied the spy."

"Meaning me, right?"

"That's right."

"We'll deal with your name-calling later, Basillio. For now, just tell me what you've got on Penny Motion."

"I just did a little breaking and entering," he said, chuckling evilly.

"Tony, you didn't! You didn't break into her apartment! You couldn't have!"

"Take it easy. I'm kidding."

"For god sakes, Tony. Will you tell me what happened—please!"

"Okay. I *did* break and enter. But not her house. It was her purse."

"What?"

"Yeah. It was kind of dumb luck, I guess. I was tailing her this afternoon and then I screwed up. I lost her. In Bergdorf's.

"So I went into this bar on Fifty-seventh Street to have a drink. And who should walk in twenty minutes later but Ms. Motion. She was having lunch with a girlfriend who works at the store. Well, she spotted me—"

I groaned.

"Just a minute. Just wait a minute. Like I said, she spotted me and asked me to join them. What could I do? Her friend left and Penny and I stayed on for another half an hour. When she went to the can, I popped open her bag and made a quick survey. Wanna know what I found?"

"You know I do."

"I found, among the pressed powder and the tampons and the green lipstick and the bank ID, a big fat check. For seventy-five hundred bucks. Made out to Ms. Motion. Signed by one Hector Naciemento."

"I see."

"Yeah. And something else interesting, too. A business card."

"What's so interesting about a business card?"

"It was her card."

"What do you mean?"

"It said 'Penelope Motion—Designer—

Clothes for the New Age' and it had an address all the way west on Fourteenth Street."

Basillio reached into his pants pocket and produced a sheet from a notepad, on which he had written the 14th Street address.

"And we thought she was a no-brain makeup girl, right? A bimbo."

"I don't use words like that, Basillio," I said halfheartedly. I was trying to make sense of it. I didn't understand what it all meant, but I knew that what Tony had uncovered was important.

The obvious explanation was that Hector was not only two-timing Grace Ann but fleecing her as well, in order to support his younger lover. But I didn't have quite enough facts to be certain about that.

And, much more important, even if our worst suspicions about Hector were true—and they very likely were—that might have nothing to do with Niles Wiegel's death. At least the connection between the two things was not apparent to me.

We had finished Tony's wine with the last serving of veal. When I placed the bowl of fruit in front of him, calling it dessert, he turned up his nose at it and set about opening the other bottle.

Tony was still preening over his discoveries.

"Pretty proud of yourself, aren't you?" I said.

"Well, aren't you? I told you your business was nasty, didn't I? I didn't do anything you wouldn't have done if you had the chance."

I had no comeback.

We had talked all night about the case and all the parties involved. It was past eleven now. The evening had vanished and I hadn't even begun my interrogation of Tony about his "problems."

That was going to have to wait for another day. I had to get to bed soon. In the morning I was going to be invaded by the fashion locusts.

Perhaps I should have put away all the dishes and scrubbed the cat box and given myself a facial and put new sheets on the bed. But I didn't. If Fliss Francis wanted a tousled, morning-after ambience, he was going to have it.

No, I wasn't going to knock myself out preparing for company tomorrow. And one thing was damn sure. I wasn't going to be serving any paté.

# Chapter 8

Bushy stood next to me, just like a little footman.

As each person entered the loft, he would look up expectantly, sure that as soon as he was noticed the adoration would start. Perhaps he thought that all the people and cameras were there to launch his new career as a film star. I don't know. But when a consumptive young girl in tight black jeans came in carrying a load of thick black cable and accidentally stepped on Bushy's tail . . . Well, he gave up. He ran screeching into the rear of the loft, and in a few seconds I heard all the signs of a scrap between him and Pancho, taking place, I think, in the basket where I keep my sweaters.

I had seen neither hide nor hair of Pancho since the first peal of the bell at nine-forty that morning.

It got to be ten-thirty. The boy genius had not yet arrived, and some of us began to talk about his tardiness on the last occasion when we were all together—the day Niles died. The conversations were getting downright morbid, actually.

I could barely remember Fliss Francis's name, let alone what he looked like. He had arrived at the Wiegels' loft just minutes after I found Niles dead in the kitchen. The rest of that day was a haze of sirens and policemen and crying and frantic phone calls.

Now here we all were again, waiting for Fliss. No corpses so far. And then the doorbell went off once more.

It wasn't Fliss. It was Sidney Rickover with an armload of fresh-cut flowers.

"I thought you were in Denver," I said in a scolding fashion as he handed one of the bouquets to me.

He was flushed and happy. "I was, briefly. We finished early, so I cut the visit short. I was glad to get out of there. Too many mountains. It depresses me."

The poor love-struck man had totally forgotten that I wanted an appointment with him. It was obvious that this high-powered lawyer was so hopelessly in love with virginal Samantha that all sense—legal and otherwise—had left him.

Sidney was a handsome man, after a fashion. He was wearing a light, beautifully tailored sports jacket that was just a little too young for him.

His graying hair had been styled, very discreetly. Everything about him seemed to say *Look at me. I'm successful, civilized, and fit.*

In some odd way, he reminded me of Felix Drinnan, Alison's companion. They were both professionals. Sidney was a lawyer and Felix a psychiatrist, although most of his psychiatric work consisted of consulting with various accreditation boards as to the training of other psychiatrists.

Each man was passionately in love with a particular woman. Each seemed to devote much of his energy and a great deal of his income to pleasing that woman.

But there, I realized, the similarity ended.

Felix's love for Alison was reciprocated. I had no idea how much, but she was living with him and she did seem to look out for him.

Sidney's love for Samantha, however, seemed to be totally rejected by her. And since it appeared he could not take no for an answer—that he would keep bringing her flowers unto all eternity—he ended up the fool.

I wondered how I would react if a man became totally enamored of me and I wasn't interested in him.

Oh, something like that scenario had happened to me many times. Particularly when I taught drama classes at the university level.

But it was always a younger man who fell head over heels in love with me.

Never an older, established, affluent man like Sidney or Felix.

If I were in Samantha's shoes, would I string him along, as she obviously did, and just keep collecting his gifts and using him?

Or would I be compassionate and end it?

A thought popped into my head: perhaps Samantha wasn't even aware of her cruelty to Sidney. Perhaps she didn't realize that she was turning Sidney into a sad, sad fool.

Then the bell rang again.

At last the great Fliss Francis was standing before me. He was exactly my height and exactly my coloring. He was no blond, though. The ends of his long auburn hair were frosted red and he was wearing a black velvet cape. There was about him an undeniable air of old-fashioned foppery.

I loved him!

From the minute he blew through the doorway like cool, leaf-laden wind, I liked him. I don't know why.

He had the smiley, goofy face of a sweet young boy destined not to live very long; his ears were much too large for his head, and his eyelashes long enough to be the envy of any woman. These he batted at me from beneath the old corduroy newsboy's cap he was wearing—its peak facing front, in contravention of the current mania for hats worn backward. There were numberless canvas and leather knapsacks dangling off every inch of his lanky frame.

And on his arm, wearing a Russian sable and black sneakers, was a young woman with one of the most recognizable faces in the world. From L.A. to Australia, her face and form—both breathtaking—adorned magazines and newspapers; she sold thousand-dollar-a-shoe shoes, snob appeal gin, deluxe automobiles, crazy new men's fragrances . . . everything. Not to mention her ubiquitousness on the couture runways in London, New York, Paris, and Milan.

She was that distinctly '90s thing, a "supermodel."

She was six foot one inch Hedy Rice, the amazing-looking girl who had become an inescapability for anyone who leafed through a magazine in the dentist's office, or read the papers with Sunday morning coffee, or followed the gossip pages in the tabloids. I did those things seldom enough, but even I knew that Hedy's father was a retired diplomat from Senegal and her British mother, a kind of absentminded professor, was a reluctant noblewoman.

Surprise number two: Hedy and Fliss were engaged to be married! Now that one *really* threw me.

"Yes! Married!" he announced ringingly, and every soul in the room flew to the two betrothed, chirping and flapping and surrounding the couple like twittering canaries.

Lord, it looked like something out of *Snow White*.

I was dumbfounded by it all—feeling very mueh out of my element. The rules had changed somewhere along the line, and they'd forgotten to tell me about it. Why would a famous young photographer who moved like a ballerina and dressed like Oscar Wilde marry a kind of hyper-woman? A female icon. A woman whose body was a sort of shrine to female sexuality. More to the point, why would he marry *any* woman?

Sex. Sexual identity. Man. Woman. Gay. Not gay. Perhaps none of that mattered in today's world. At least, not in this little world I'd become involved with as of late. Maybe in this tight little community, the only thing that mattered was that you were *fabulous.*

Oh, well. I was by turn bewildered, amused, and really turned off by these people. But I still liked Fliss.

I looked over at Basillio, who had been assigned the task of finding electrical outlets for all the equipment. He seemed just as happy this time as the last to play a small part in the goings-on. I thought he was taking special pleasure in ogling the lovely Miss Eugenie Putnam, who along with her striking, silver-haired mother, was being photographed in white gauze pajamas, which the harsh lights in the room rendered absolutely transparent.

Tony asked me if I wanted him to go in and make coffee for the crowd. Absolutely not, I told him. Anybody who wanted breakfast—even so much as a tea bag—had to call and order it up from the deli on Greenwich. We weren't going to have any more toxic food incidents if I could help it.

By the time Fliss started to work in earnest, around eleven-thirty, Hedy was gone. A stretch limo had pulled up at the curb and whisked her away to a talk-show taping.

They had taken off all of Alison's makeup. She was being posed in the window near my bed, which had been un-made and rumpled badly, to suggest a night without sleep, I suppose. Her hair had that up-and-down, wisps and curls, roll-in-the-hayloft quality. That quality had taken thirty-five minutes to achieve; during that time I had to stand motionless at the foot of the bed, a fake cup of tea in my hands, which I was to hold out consolingly to Alison.

Don't ask me what the picture was supposed to mean. I trusted the judgment of Fliss Francis—as the Collins sisters obviously did—that women looking at this odd, arty shot would be moved to buy the short, beaded white dresses we were wearing.

While we were waiting for lunch to be delivered, I became aware of how few words the Collins sisters had actually spoken to me during the day. Only when I had to be pinned or padded or when it was time to change outfits did Samantha speak to me. Grace Ann had reintroduced Fliss and me ever so briefly when he first arrived—managing, miraculously, not to mention that he and I had first met over Niles's dead body, so to speak. Since then, Grace Ann and Samantha had both avoided me like measles.

Fliss didn't seem constrained by any such delicacy. Getting along famously, he and I were sitting by ourselves in the window where Alison had struck attitude after attitude with her perfectly swollen little lips.

He said "the buzz" was that Niles did not die accidentally, and he asked me outright if I thought anybody was going to get bumped off today.

"I'm doing what I can to prevent that," I told him.

"If you ask me," he said a few minutes later, "whoever it was that did Niles in should have taken that goddamn cat of his along too. I mean, after all, darling, that's the way Niles would have wanted it. Since he was so fond of the bloody beast."

"You know Bobbin?"

"Oh God, yes. Damn bear. But then, I suppose I'm prejudiced. Never got along with cats. They're such selfish, vicious things."

Oh. Fliss Francis was rapidly losing points with me.

"No wonder I don't like them," he went on. "They're much too much like me."

Okay. That kind of self-awareness put a few points back on his side of the ledger.

"So, Fliss, you know the whole story of how Bobbin wound up at Niles and Lainie's."

"Every preposterous detail. Why?"

"I'm just dying to know."

"Really? What on earth for? I must have misjudged you, darling Alice. I didn't think your life was so dull that you'd be interested in—Oh, wait! I get it! You're the actress, aren't you? You're going to study them . . . or something . . . the Collins ladies, I mean."

I neither confirmed not denied Fliss's assumption. Instead, I merely smiled.

He went on. "Well, dearest, the problem with little Bobbin started not long after Grace Ann and Hector became—oh, how does she put it?"

"Friends," I supplied.

"Yes, that's it. Friends. 'Lovely friends.' I mean, *puhl-leeeze*! Anyway, Hector began spending a few nights a week at Grace Ann and Samantha's place. After this lovely friendship had been going for a while, Hector told Grace Ann he had developed an allergy to cat hair.

"Allergic to Bobbin? she says. Well then, out the little monster goes, on his ass. Anything for a friend—right? Especially when he's got dimples to die for and a body by Jake. Right, darling? I mean, right?"

Fliss tossed his curls back over one shoulder.

"And Samantha stood by without protesting?"

"Protest? She did everything but tie herself to the front of a train. But to no avail. Grace Ann was determined to find another home for darling Bobbin at the earliest possible moment. Samantha's attitude that Bobbin was like her own child cut absolutely no ice with Grace Ann, who was, after all, a woman in . . . lovely friendship."

Fliss laughed wickedly. "The two of them, oh, the two of them! I'm convinced there's some sort of *Whatever Happened to Baby Jane* secret sort of thing going on there. Especially in Sam's case. But God, can that woman cut velvet! She's a genius, isn't she?"

"Yes she is. So what happened after Samantha couldn't change Grace Ann's mind about the cat?"

"Oh, Sam got a temporary reprieve—or rather Bobbin did. They couldn't find anybody to take in the hoary old monster. Not even Grace Ann would turn him out into the street. She'd promised Sam that she wouldn't get rid of Bobbin until a good home could be found for him. But there were no takers. Until, that is—"

"Until Niles."

"Yes, until Niles. Who not only consented to take the poor beast in but planned to devote his life to Bobbin. He just loved him to pieces. He stood ready, willing, and able to provide a home for the cat. And he confided in Samantha first. The fool!

"Well, Samantha begged him not to tell this to Hector and Grace Ann. But he insisted. He had to have his Bobbin. And so he did."

"And Samantha despised him because of it," I filled in.

"Yes. Despised. To put it mildly."

"In fact," I said, "she must have hated him more than she did Hector, who started it all by complaining about the cat."

"Isn't it pathetically sick-making? Isn't it whimsical beyond all tolerance?"

"I don't know, Fliss. A person can become fanatically attached to an animal. Sometimes they prove to be truer friends than . . . friends."

"Well, I maintain it's twisted. Still, for a while there Samantha behaved as though part of her heart had been cut out or something. Life was over for her. Imagine it! Someone who lives not ten yards from Eighth Avenue—good Lord, someone born in your Mississippi—and all she cares about is—"

He had stopped abruptly.

"What?" I asked. "What were you going to say, Fliss?"

"How unimportant that is now, dear. I just realized what I was doing."

"What do you mean? What were you doing?"

Lydia Adamson

"Sending poor daft Samantha to prison for murder, aren't I?"

He regarded me expectantly.

We broke again for tea. At about four-thirty that afternoon.

Then we worked till seven-forty in the evening. I hadn't seen Pancho and Bushy in hours. I could only guess how mad they were going to be about all this.

I thought the fashion locusts would never leave. But finally they did.

Only Alison and Tony remained. My niece was standing at a window on the far side of the loft. She was staring out moodily.

"Alison, are you watching for Felix?" I assumed he would pick her up and take her to dinner.

She didn't answer. She didn't respond at all. I walked over to her.

"Alison! What's the matter?"

She wheeled suddenly and flung herself sobbing into my arms. I didn't know what to do, so I just held her.

Then she relaxed her hold and stepped back.

"Is it Felix?" I asked.

She shook her head no.

"Is it something that happened during the shoot?" I pressed. Her misery was intense—that was obvious.

Again she shook her head no. She held up

one hand, signifying that as soon as she got her crying under control she would tell me.

I waited. She was lovely, even in misery. Her hair was now cut short, but when I looked at her I always saw the incredibly long golden hair. Like her mother's. Like my poor sister's hair. Rapunzel hair, my grandmother used to call it. One could let it fall from a castle window so that a lover could ascend.

"I feel so rotten," she finally said.

"Why?"

"Because I've been so terrible to you, Aunt Alice. So damn neglectful."

"What on earth are you talking about?"

She grabbed my hand. "Do you remember how wonderful it was when we discovered each other on that movie set in France?"

"I will never forget it."

"Nor will I. Because it was a miracle. Things like that just don't happen. And it was even more wonderful and miraculous that you took me back to the States. And gave me a family again. And a place to live." She paused and squeezed my hand hard.

"But what did I do to repay you, Aunt Alice? I'll tell you what I did. Not a damn thing. I didn't help you with your cat-sitting business. I was useless in your investigation of that poor young woman who was murdered when she came to help with Pancho. And to top it all off—the minute Felix asked me to move in with him, I abandoned you."

She balled her hands into fists and added: "I didn't even feed your cats!"

I looked past her and could see Tony trying to be discreet . . . trying not to hear.

Then, as is my wont in difficult situations, I made a totally frivolous remark.

I said: "A supermodel's life is no picnic."

I had no idea why that popped into my head. Or what it meant. Or whether I was trying to be funny.

But Alison just stared at me for a moment. Then she broke into hysterical laughter. So did I.

The situation was defused.

After the hilarity died down, Alison said: "I'm sorry I carried on like that."

"There's nothing to be sorry about."

"It was this shoot. It unhinged me."

"You mean it was a bit too much?"

"More than a bit, Aunt Alice. It was intoxicating. I mean it was astonishing. All these beautiful people hovering around us like we were rare jewels. And the makeup and the lights and the . . . Well, anyway, when it was all over and everybody started leaving, it was like the ball was over. You know what I mean?"

"Yes, I know. Fashion is a branch of theater."

"So I slipped into a sudden depression. With a whoosh. But now I'm fine."

I kissed her on the forehead. Then I quipped: "When you and I are both rich and famous as the Camisole Queens, we'll keep a shrink on our staff. To attend to us after each shoot. Not Felix, mind you. I mean an old-fashioned Freudian."

"And a masseuse," she added.

"Of course."

"And a chef."

"And a footman."

That confused me. "Why a footman?"

"To serve us cheese and wine."

"Why not?"

"And a bootmaker."

"Why not?"

"Every famous model should have her own bootmaker."

"A Corsican," I offered.

"Yes. Definitely a Corsican. A tall, slender young man with powerful hands. He looks tubercular. But he really isn't. He lives to make elegant boots."

She paused in her fantasy and then said something to me in French. Alison often lapsed into French when she was excited or stressed. I didn't understand what she said. It showed on my face.

"I'm sorry. I asked you if you think we'll make *Vogue*."

"Why not?"

"Just the American *Vogue*?"

"Maybe the French *Vogue*, too."

"Let me see—how many are there?" she wondered aloud.

"I don't know. There's also a British

*Vogue.* And a German *Vogue.* And an Italian *Vogue.*"

"What about Albania? Do they have a *Vogue*?"

"I don't know."

"Poor Albania," she said. Then she kissed me, turned sharply, and headed toward the door, swaying in an exaggerated rendition of the fashion model's runway walk.

I watched her leave. I was becoming weary.

A supermodel's life is no picnic.

I took two cold beers out of the refrigerator and offered one to Tony. To my surprise, he declined.

"I've got to run, Swede."

"Oh? But I have a meat loaf—"

"Tomorrow. I'll eat it cold."

"And I haven't had the chance to tell you what I found out about Bobbin and the Wiegels."

"Gotta run, Swede." He was already fiddling with the front door lock.

"Where are you going in such a hurry, Tony?"

"Gotta make a curtain. A friend got tickets."

"Oh, okay. So run."

"Bye. Tomorrow for part two of the Motion caper, too," Tony's voice trailed back to me as he went out the door.

I stared after him in bewilderment.

"That means I'll keep following Penny," he

called back over his shoulder. "So long, Swede."

While I drank the ale, I wondered what I would do if I fell deeply, passionately, hopelessly in love with a man who was allergic to cats. It seemed an insoluble problem, until I decided that I could not ever love a man who was allergic to cats. It was that simple.

Oddly enough, I didn't find Samantha's hatred for Niles so improbable, given the circumstances.

Oddly enough, I found myself thinking of dozens of devious ways of revenging myself on someone who took away an animal I had loved and lived with for many years.

I indulged in those violent fantasies for quite a few minutes before a sense of shame set in.

I opened that other bottle of beer.

From out of nowhere, Pancho came zooming up onto the sofa. Bushy followed a minute later, only he sat in my lap and visited awhile. Together we watched Pancho sniffing out his enemies—in the shadows, behind the stove, on top of the counters.

By the time I was ready for bed, there was little doubt in my mind that Samantha Collins had killed Niles Wiegel. No matter how crazy her motive might sound to an outsider.

I was all but sure of it.

The trouble was, I hadn't the vaguest idea what to do about it.

\* \* \*

The telephone woke me from a rather interesting dream. In it, I was only one part of Fliss Francis's vast harem, for whom Samantha and Grace Ann Collins did all the sewing. It was my wedding day. But I was also scheduled for beheading. Grace Ann was explaining why the dress they'd sold me was such a practical purchase to have made.

Three-thirty in the morning! Who the hell was calling me at this hour? On the way across the room to pick up the phone. I started posing possible answers to that question. Three-thirty A.M. calls were invariably bad news. Invariably. Three-thirty A.M. meant the worst kind of trouble.

I picked up the receiver cautiously.

"Cat Woman? Hello, are you there?"

"Who is this?" I asked.

"You don't know who this is, Cat Woman?"

"Rothwax? Rothwax, is this you?"

"That's right. The very one."

"Why on earth are you calling me at three-thirty in the morning?"

"What does time matter to a feline spirit like yourself? Don't you prowl all night?"

"Tell me, have you lost your mind, Lieutenant Rothwax?"

"Call me anything. But don't call me 'lieutenant.' I'm *Mister* Rothwax now. Got a new job. I'm director of security for the Korean Merchants Association."

"You're kidding. You left the Department?"

"Did you think I never would?"

"I think you're calling because you need help."

"Somebody does. But it ain't me."

"What are you talking about, Rothwax?"

"I just got a call from your friend Anthony."

*"Basillio?"*

"Right. He's being held for questioning by Manhattan North detectives."

"Questioning about what?"

"A murder."

I went cold then. "Go on," I was finally able to say.

"Looks like he was shacking up with this young girl, Penny Motion. He let himself into her apartment a little past midnight. Claims she was already dead when he got there. He found her on the bathroom floor, he says, strangled with a towel. He dropped my name to one of the cops at Manhattan North. Guy calls me and says Basillio wants me to get in touch with you."

I thanked Rothwax for his help and wished him well in his new job—that is, I think I did. I'm not sure. I just knew my mouth was so dry that my throat ached.

I needed two things now. They kept going around and around in my head. I saw them spelled out in bright cartoon letters: WATER and STRENGTH.

I needed water and strength. Strength and water.

But they both seemed such a long way off. And I could not get my legs to move.

# Chapter 9

"I wish you would go ahead and shoot me or something."

I said nothing.

The detectives had released Tony at seven A.M. He and I had stumbled blindly out of the station house and into the first cab we saw. We had sat numbly in the backseat, all the questions, the accusations, the anger bubbling under the surface, just waiting to erupt.

Now we were back at the loft. The dappled morning sun and the seductive autumn breeze seemed to mock us with their loveliness.

"I'm not kidding. Go ahead!" he said pitifully. "I'd rather have you shoot me than keep on looking at me that way."

"Don't give me that choice again, Tony. I might just take you up on it," I said.

"How many times do you want me to say I'm sorry, huh?"

"I don't want you to say it at all, Tony. I don't want to hear it. And you know why?"

I didn't give him a chance to answer.

"Because you're apologizing for the wrong thing, Tony, that's why. If you wanted to have a fling with that girl, it was your business. We're not married and I don't have a leash around your neck. No! It's for what you did to me as a . . . a comrade . . . a colleague . . . that I'm so furious at you. You *lied* to me. You deceived me. You lied about how you got that information on Penny. And you compromised this investigation. You threw everything off! Don't you understand that?"

"But everything I told you about Penny was true. The check from Naciemento. The weird business card. Everything."

"Yes. Except you didn't peek into her handbag in any bar, did you? You looked while she was in the shower or something."

"Something like that," he said contritely.

"Looks like you weren't very honest with Penny either. You slept with her but you betrayed her, too. You *spied on her,* didn't you? You lied to her. You used her. Just like you accused me of doing. As a matter of fact, everything you accused me of, you were guilty of yourself. Isn't that true, Tony?"

He looked away from me.

I could sense what he was feeling. What he was seeing. A young woman grotesquely twisted. The knotted towel. The sudden vision of death. The end of love. The end of everything for Penny Motion. I could sense what he needed now—compassion. But it wouldn't come from me—not now.

"Isn't it true?" I demanded. "You played her for a fool just as you played me for a fool."

"That's crazy and you know it!" he bellowed. "I've never played you for a fool, never. And I went after Penny because I dug her. That's all. I wanted her and I couldn't help myself. But I didn't play her for a fool either."

"No. It was the other way around, I suppose."

"What other way around?"

I began to laugh caustically. "I mean that Penny made rather a fool of you, didn't she? You've already admitted that you started sleeping with her the very first night you ever met her—after Niles was killed. So you must have been in a state of shock that day when you saw her with Hector. I bet you felt like a fool then, didn't you? How did you keep yourself from running over there and making a scene?"

"Like you said, I don't—didn't—have a leash on her."

"Right! And you also knew that Hector would have knocked your block off."

"Don't be so damn sure I'm such a weakling, Swede. Such a schmuck. Maybe if you had a higher opinion of me—"

"Maybe what? What, Tony? Maybe *I'm* to blame for your pathetic midlife panic—for your silly lust for a girl half your age? Is that what you were going to say? It's my fault? Because I haven't treated you like the macho he-man you are? Haven't appreciated you enough."

"Haven't loved me enough," he corrected, bitterness in every syllable.

"Oh, come off it. I thought we understood each other about that."

And indeed I did think that Basillio and I had long ago reached an agreement about it. Tony tended to profess love a bit too easily. And to be terribly wounded when I didn't return his feelings with the same intensity.

There's love and then there's love, I had once told him.

I also told him I thought we had something better than that all-consuming passion he seemed to need, better than the starry-eyed, youthful kind of love he was talking about. We were friends. We had a history together. And we were lovers. Even if other affairs intervened, some of them serious, Basillio and I always came back together.

"Maybe *you* understood, Swede. And with you, that's all that counts. Things have always been a little one-sided where you're concerned. You have to call the shots."

"All right, Tony! That's enough! No more corny sports metaphors and no more talking about us. About me, anyway."

"See? See what I mean? *You've* decided

that the discussion about us is finished. So it's finished."

"It *is* finished, Basillio. Because it's unimportant now. You don't seem to realize what kind of trouble you could be in."

"Like hell I don't! I know the cops would like to tie things up real neat by making me say I killed that girl. I know I could be in deep shit. But what am I supposed to do—thank you again for helping me out with the cops and the attorney and Rothwax and all the rest of it? Am I supposed to get down on my knees?"

"No, idiot! You're supposed to help me find out who's killing these people. And now I don't think you can.

"You're hardly an objective party in the investigation now. Just as you couldn't be objective when you were 'gathering evidence' on your own lover. Don't you see," I began to shriek at him, "you've become a suspect, you—Oh God, Tony!"

"I swear I didn't kill Penny."

He grasped my arm then, desperate, and repeated, "I didn't kill her!"

"Don't you think I know that?" I snapped at him, throwing his hand off me. And then was immediately sorry. There was such pain and fear in his voice.

"Listen, Tony, it's been a long horrible day—and night—or night and day—whatever. You've been through a police grilling, You're exhausted and so am I."

"Yeah," Tony said flatly. "We need sleep. The both of us."

He stood and wearily flexed his arms. I saw him gaze longingly over at my bed.

"Not here, Tony. Not this time."

"Okay."

He seemed to take forever to reach the front door. And when he finally did, he turned back toward me, eyes downcast. "Look, Swede—"

"Just don't call me that right now, Tony."

"All right. When can I call you that again?"

"After we clear you . . . maybe."

"All right. But look, I want you to understand—it wasn't serious with her, you know. I mean, it might have been, but I didn't . . . All I'm trying to say is I still love you."

"Don't, Tony."

"What do you mean—don't love you or don't say it?"

"Just don't! Just go!"

And he did.

But I ran out and caught up with him. I kissed him on the forehead and then waited until his footsteps died away on the stairs.

I needed sleep, it was true. But I couldn't sleep.

I paced for a long while. I fed the cats and showered and made coffee and put on the radio, to see if there'd be a news item on Penny Motion's murder.

Just yesterday, I'd been traipsing around the loft like a fool in those airy costumes. So much had changed in a mere twenty-four hours.

What a difference a day makes, as the song goes. Just yesterday, I was operating on the theory that Samantha Collins had poisoned Niles Wiegel because he'd taken Bobbin away from her. Right now, that idea seemed pretty damn foolish, too. It now seemed clear that Niles's death and Penny's death were of a piece.

The key to Niles's death lay not in his relationship to a big bear of a cat but to one of the other people in this crooked circle of friends and colleagues. Or maybe more than one.

Niles and Penny. Niles and Hector. Niles and Lainie. Niles and the Collins sisters. Which pairing had led to that deathly still body draped across the kitchen counter? Which pairing had triggered the brutal strangulation of young Penny Motion?

And then there was the even bigger question. The most frightening one of all: Would the murdering stop at two? Or were other members of the circle marked for death?

Meanwhile, solving Penny's murder had taken on double importance. I had to help clear Basillio. I didn't know if I could ever forgive him for playing odds against the middle with me and Penny and the investigation. But I never doubted for an instant that Tony was innocent of the murder.

These fashion-obsessed people were an odd lot, to put it mildly. I was convinced that each member of the circle was hiding something—that each had something to protect—some secret. In fact, there seemed to be no end to their secrets.

At least I had made one new friend who didn't seem to have anything to hide. The friendship wasn't a long-standing one—only twenty-four hours old. But I was going to have to take my new friend into my confidence.

I'd made stranger alliances in my life, I'm sure. But I was damned if I could think of one any stranger than Fliss Francis.

# Chapter 10

I must have let the phone ring twenty times. There was no answer at Samantha and Grace Ann's brownstone. So I tried the shop.

I had done my share of fibbing and manipulating Julia, the shop assistant. Now the tables were turned.

She would tell me nothing until I gave her the lowdown on my friend Tony Basillio and Penny and the whole shocking scandal. And of course she *had* to know about Hedy Rice's brief appearance at the session.

It was only after I'd described the Jean Paul Gaultier that Hedy was wearing, and her newest haircut, only after I swore that she was just as astonishingly gorgeous in the flesh as on the printed page, that Julia told me Fliss usually stayed at the Pierre when he was in town. Either there, or the Hotel Chelsea.

Also, Julia told me, I was wasting my time calling Grace Ann and Samantha. The Collinses had unplugged their phone. They were speaking to no one. Hector had been detained by the police and apparently the experience was shattering. He was upstairs resting and could not be disturbed.

Thankfully, Fliss had gone for downtown chic rather than uptown luxe. He was at the Chelsea.

I jumped into the only clothing I could lay my hands on that was both clean and right at hand—black jeans and oversized white shirt.

Oh, yes, and my ancient raincoat. Because it was pouring. Which turned out to be a lucky break for me. Fliss was scheduled to shoot some outdoor scenes for a client that day, and he'd had to cancel because of the weather.

Last, I put on the old pair of sturdy men's lace-ups that had once belonged to my ex-husband. Strangely enough, we wore the same size shoe. But that was not why we got married, any more than it explained why we didn't stay married.

Fliss had taken a suite at the Chelsea. Large bedroom, musty old sitting room with fireplace, kitchenette, ancient bathtub with clawfoot tub, arched doorways everywhere, threadbare carpets. All of it appropriately grimy around the edges. It fairly dripped with faded elegance.

One of the skinny young girls from the photo session showed me in. Fliss was waiting for me in a blue satin smoking jacket.

"I thoroughly approve of that outfit, darling," he said when I peeled off my coat.

I looked down in puzzlement at the things I had so hastily thrown on.

"Oh yes!" he exclaimed. "The Kate Hepburn look suits you to a tee. And those shoes, my dear . . . brilliant touch. I think Samantha was utterly wrong when she said you had no taste."

"Your rooms are charming, Fliss," I said.

"Aren't they twee?" he agreed.

"Aren't they what?"

"*Twee*, darling. You know. Oh, that's right. I keep forgetting you're not English. It just means . . . oh, cozy . . . just right . . . or something like that. But never mind that now. Get in here this minute and tell me all!"

Yes, I planned to do just that. And, I was hoping that Fliss would return the favor.

He took me by the shoulders and plopped me down in an old red plush armchair.

"My Lord!" he cried. "Imagine waking up to this!" Fliss waved a newspaper madly through the air. It was the early edition of the *Post*. "Our little set is the talk of the bloody town, darling. Penny Motion killed in a *crime passionel*! How fabulously sordid. And, of course, how awful for you."

"Me? Why me?"

"Well, Mr. Basillio was your bit of it, wasn't he? Your squeeze. And now he's part of a love-nest killing and he didn't even give you the courtesy of making you the victim. You aren't even *mentioned* in the story, poor lamb."

"Exactly who was mentioned?"

"The victim, of course. Mr. Basillio. Hector. The Sisters Collins. And, it goes without saying, my betrothed and *moi*. They told how Penny was assisting at a photographic session earlier in the day. And they ran the most unfortunate photo of the child. So unflattering it was practically libelous. I mean, she must have lost a ton of weight after that photo was taken. It doesn't do her the least justice. Oh, well, isn't it all absolutely hideous—in a thrilling sort of way?"

"I'd rather get my thrills from a roller coaster, Fliss. And I hate roller coasters. Besides, I know Tony didn't do it."

"She knows he didn't do it," he said, batting those eyelashes again. And then he broke into song—*"he was her man, but he was doing her wrong."*

"Fliss, you are truly outrageous."

"Well, of course I am, sweetie! Who do you think you're dealing with here?"

"Someone I can trust, I think. I hope. I've got to get Tony out from under this charge . . . and find out the truth about Niles Wiegel's death as well. I think you can help me."

"How?"

"You know Grace Ann and Samantha."

"Yes."

"You know Hector."

"Yes."

"You knew Niles and Lainie."

"Yes. Well, not her so much."

"Fliss, I've got to dig into this list, because surely one of them killed Niles and then Penny."

"Based on our little tête-à-tête the other day, darling, I'd say you've already decided it was Sam."

"That was a momentary flight. I was thinking that Samantha had gone off the deep end and killed Niles because of the episode with Bobbin. But Penny's murder took care of that theory."

"And so who's the present little canary in the cage? Out with it, Inspector. Who done it?"

"Hector looks awfully good for it," I said. "He was sleeping with Penny."

Fliss hooted with laughter. "Yes, indeed. Poaching on your boyfriend's estate, eh? Well, I can't say it's a surprise, dearie. Jezebel must be beside herself."

"Who's Jezebel? Oh, you mean Grace Ann. Yes, I imagine she must be."

"Well, there you have it, Alice. There's your motive. Grace Ann found out about the affair and killed Penny in the proverbial jealous rage."

"Don't think that hasn't occurred to me. But I'm sure the same person is responsible for both deaths. And I can't assign her a motive for killing Niles."

"Oh. I see. Well, as far as Hector's concerned—not that I'm looking to defend him—but I can't imagine him killing anyone over a little dalliance. If he found out that Penny and your mister were having it off, I think he'd be more amused than enraged."

"Yes. You may be right about that. On the other hand, how can you really know how Hector would react if he found out that *he* was the one being double-timed, for a change? All his sophistication might have abandoned him.

"Plus, Hector's relationship with Niles was complicated, it seems. They went back a long way, but lately they were quarreling bitterly. That is, if I can trust the person who gave me that information. Something in the past might explain why he would kill Niles.

"That's why I need to go into their past a bit. You knew Niles before his marriage. When he and Hector were in business together. They had a restaurant. What do you know about that partnership?"

"Oh dear. Not much. It was around the time that the business was failing when I met them. We were introduced by the bloke who was their chef of the moment. He worked as a caterer sometimes. That is how one knew him. And when he began cooking at Niles and Hector's cafe, he put the word out to everyone in the business."

"Who was this bloke—chef?"

"Oh, a very colorful character, also from your American South. Brewer was his name. Brewer Bloodworth."

"Any idea where I can find him now?"

"More than an idea, darling. Oh, I tell you, fate is a strange thing!"

"Why?"

"Hedy has a chum named Lois. Another model. We just adore Lois. Good with hats. Fabulous figure for swimsuits. And loves to eat—she's a famous bulemic, you know. Anyhoo, just a few days ago Lois told us about a new place to eat. She said we must go there before the whole world discovers it. And it just so happens that the chef is one Brewer Bloodworth."

"What's this restaurant called?"

"Oh, damn. I forget. But Hedy will remember. We'll take you there."

"Good. I'd appreciate it. What about tonight?"

"Fabulous! My dear, the excitement!"

"Just one thing, Fliss."

"Of course."

"You can't tell anyone I'm nosing around this way. I'm serious about finding this killer. And Tony's freedom may depend on it."

"Look at my lips, darling. See these lips? Sealed."

"Thank you, Fliss."

"Now I have one thing to ask of you, too."

"What?" I said.

He looked at me very sternly. "I want it firmly understood when you're playing William Powell tonight that *I* am Myrna Loy."

Traffic was bad. We got out of the cab and began to walk. No small feat for Hedy, whose pumps must have measured six or seven inches high.

Hair slicked back, shoulders and midriff bare, thighs of wonder straining against her black Lycra miniskirt, Hedy was not doing a bad job of stopping traffic herself.

We were not far from the enduringly glamorous Flatiron Building, in that constantly mutating district between Chelsea, to the west, and Gramercy Park, to the east.

Because of a spate of new restaurants featuring celebrated chefs or celebrity owners, the Flatiron district is currently a mecca for restaurant thrill seekers. Much of the credit for this is owed to the magazines and the columnists in the daily papers, who whip potential customers into a frenzy to spend three hundred dollars on a meal for two, merely by hinting that some high-profile media hog dines regularly at a certain restaurant.

Hedy's friend Lois had advised her to have a meal in Brewer Bloodworth's new restaurant before the rest of the world discovered it. It was a little late for that.

Fliss, Hedy, and I stepped in through the silvered doors of High Tide, which specialized in Pacific Rim cuisine, according to the menu posted in the entryway.

The big room was bursting with people. They stood three abreast at the bar. They lounged on pretty little divans at the front of the restaurant. They were squeezed into the area between the bar and the dining room. They waited in little knots in the alcove near the bathrooms.

Yet, in less than thirty seconds, our party was being shown to a choice table. I suppose Fliss had called Chef Bloodworth to say he and Hedy would be dining tonight, and the staff had been put on alert to roll out the red—or in this case, plum-colored—carpet. Clout. Social power. So this is what it felt like. It gave me the creeps, frankly.

Every eye in the place seemed to follow us across the floor. I knew the people were watching Hedy, not me, but it made me incredibly uncomfortable. I had no trouble performing for hundreds of people in a darkened theater, every eye trained on me, but this was something else altogether.

I thought of the story another actress had told me once. She was dating a fellow actor, a wildly handsome man who, incredibly enough, was nominated for the Academy Award. On Oscar night, as they stepped out of his limousine, a phalanx of reporters quite literally knocked her off her feet in an attempt to get to him. She wound up spending the evening not in the Dorothy Chandler Pavilion but the emergency room of Cedars Sinai Hospital, her ankle smashed to bits.

I found myself laughing a little hysterically as we slid into our blackleather booth. I don't think anyone noticed, though.

How the hell was I supposed to interview Brewer Bloodworth under these circumstances? Not even William Powell could do it.

It was a long night. But at least the meal was worth it. Chef Bloodworth's food was magnificent. All sorts of mysterious herbs and weeds and shellfish I had never heard of. Rice like none I had ever tasted before. And desserts from the gods.

It was nearly one A.M. now and the restaurant, blessedly, had mostly emptied out. Fliss and Hedy were just getting revved up for the evening.

A couple they knew, one of many who had dropped by the table during the course of the evening, had invited them to a club down on Houston Street. They would all meet up, it was agreed, around two A.M.

I was ready for bed and nothing but bed. I was punchy with fatigue. But I couldn't collapse yet and I couldn't leave yet. Chef Bloodworth had agreed to see me at the end of the night.

Sitting with us now was a young woman

whose current rock song was number twelve on the charts. Her two companions, sculpted young male dancers, had done a couple of music videos with Hedy. I was sitting trancelike, half listening to their fond reminiscences, when Hedy poked me gently on the shoulder.

"You're on, girlfriend," she said.

"What?"

Hedy pointed across the room at the stumpy man with a ponytail who was talking casually to the bartender. "There's Brewer," she said.

In a blizzard of kisses—for me, for Brewer, for the rock 'n' roll trio—Fliss and Hedy soon left for their party, still attempting to cajole me into accompanying them. I thanked them for dinner, and for all their help, but finally convinced them they were wasting their breath.

Brewer Bloodworth was a surprise on many fronts. One, he didn't look as I had pictured him.

Two, he wasn't a hyper-hip egomaniac chef to the stars, bragging about the big shots he'd fed in his day. Instead, he spoke self-deprecatingly in a courtly, honeyed southern drawl, painting himself as just a good ol' boy who loved his kitchen and took his greatest pleasure in seeing folks eat well.

And three—in the biggest shock of all—he recognized me!

In fact, over the Armagnacs he insisted we share, he began to reel off a list of my stage credits going back more than ten years. He'd seen me in *Mother Courage* at the little Second Avenue theater they had torn down in '81. He'd seen my nurse in *Romeo and Juliet*. He enjoyed me in the Albert Jarry play up at Columbia and the Edward Albee on West Street. And by the way, did I still teach that class at the New School?

I nearly fell off my barstool.

According to Chef Bloodworth, it was actors like myself who were responsible for his leaving his beloved Savannah and settling in New York. He used to make regular trips "up here," being a fanatical theater devotee, and I had provided some of the most wonderful hours he'd ever been privileged to spend in the theater.

Heady stuff indeed. It took me awhile to recover my senses and begin to probe him about his experiences with Niles and Hector.

As soon as I mentioned their names, however, his face darkened and his relaxed, convivial manner disappeared.

Brewer poured another Armagnac for himself. "Miss Alice, they are two of the ugliest characters it's ever been my misfortune to meet."

"Really? Why?"

"I think it would be best to let the curtain fall on that business," he said ruefully. "That particular play is over. All I can say is that Niles Wiegel and Hector Naciemento are some very sorry examples of modern man. They pass themselves off as the new gentry, but the truth is, they're no better than street hustlers. They are, in a word, trash."

"You know, Brewer, I can't help noticing that you refer to Niles Wiegel in the present tense. You have heard, haven't you, that Niles is dead?"

He didn't answer for a moment. Then he nodded. "Yes," he said finally. "Yes. I believe I did hear that."

He might have been talking about a new model of dishwasher for all the emotion in his voice.

"About Hector—" I began.

"Is he dead, too?" Brewer asked genially.

"No. Not at all. But he was questioned recently in the investigation of a young girl's murder."

"Lovely," he said low.

"She was his lover, although Hector is currently involved with another woman, a friend of mine, actually."

"Well, Alice, you tell your friend to get as far away from that phony Brazilian scum as she can."

He paused only long enough to light a cigarette. In those few seconds, his voice had taken on a markedly different cast. "And tell her something else, baby. Tell her, before he goes out the door she better count the silverware—along with her fingers and toes."

"I don't think she would listen to me. As I said, she's in love with him."

"Honey, who hasn't been?"

I took a deep breath before asking the next question: "Were you?"

Brewer Bloodworth turned a curious kind of smile on me then. In a few seconds, his gentility was firmly back in place. "Alice, I've enjoyed our talk so very much. You have a good night now."

It was two-thirty in the morning when the taxi dropped me at home. The driver did not wait to see that I got safely indoors before he zoomed off.

I could have crawled up the stairs. That's how tired I was. I couldn't even remember the last time I'd had a night's sleep.

As I lay in bed, I turned the whole evening over in my mind. Everything from our entrance through the swinging silver doors, to the hush that fell as we followed the maître d' to our table, to all the good-looking people who'd stopped to pay homage to Fliss's fame and Hedy's beauty, to the little spot of mango ice cream I tried to sponge off the jacket of my suit.

And especially to my wee-hours chat with Brewer Bloodworth.

Something was off about Brewer Bloodworth. Something was weird.

I thought about the few chefs I'd ever met. To a person, they'd been distinctly reserved. Civil enough, once in a while they'd stop at your table to ask if you'd enjoyed the meal. But basically introverted. Brooders, really. And very hard to impress.

But Bloodworth had made an awful big fuss over me. That is, before I'd asked him one question too many and he shut me down. It was as if he thought it was important to make me like him—trust him. I couldn't imagine why.

And with that thought, all thinking ceased for the night. Sleep descended upon me, much as Brewer had said, like a curtain ringing down.

I slept till noon.

Pancho and Bushy were pretty crabby over missing their breakfast. But they had taken pity on me. They had made no attempt to wake me. For that I blessed them. And opened a can of sardines for their delectation. The vet always counsels me to put them on a diet. But the vet be damned.

Was I still dieting? Actually, I could no longer remember. So when I hit the street at one o'clock, I headed for the diner on West Street and had my fill of cream cheese on my bagel.

As I sat devouring my very late breakfast, for the first time since I'd moved into the loft I missed my old neighborhood. I missed having the waitress in the coffee shop call me by name. I missed Mrs. Oshrin, my elderly neighbor on 26th

Street. I missed the dingy shoe repair place on Second Avenue and the spotless Viennese bakery on Third.

Life had changed. Without my noticing. I hadn't had a cat-sitting assignment in a long time. And work in the theater was so scarce that it seemed almost a distant memory. I was a novice fashion model. At age forty-one. I had considered it ridiculous from the word go. Suddenly, it had become intolerable as well. And inexplicably sad.

And then there was the Basillio mess. Nothing like the Penny Motion affair had ever happened to us before. I honestly didn't know if Tony and I would ever be able to pick up the pieces of our friendship.

I asked for more coffee, drank it down quickly, and paid my check. Then I headed toward Sheridan Square. I was finally going to make a purchase at Village Cigars. As I had always heard it, there was nothing you couldn't buy there.

The item I wanted came in orange and purple. It was a tough choice, but I settled on orange. No, not a "fun" condom. I bought an eye-straining, psychedelic orange disposable camera. They took credit cards at Village Cigars. I would have to remember that.

It took a couple of hours, but at last I got my chance to photograph Brewer Bloodworth. He did not know that he was my subject. I hung about the canopied apartment building on 20th Street, across from the restaurant, until the last of the lunch-hour patrons at High Tide straggled out. Presently Brewer himself left the restaurant. And I was able to get two or three clear shots of him, full face, as he struggled into his light jacket and then paused to light a cigarette.

I dropped the film off at the super-quick-service developer on Seventh Avenue, extracting the promise from them that I could pick up my photos, enlargements and all, in two and a half hours.

So I had a little time to kill. It was during lulls like this that I'd normally have coffee or a drink somewhere with Tony. And for a minute there I was tempted to call him. But I didn't.

Instead, I went home and did the laundry in the streamlined machine I had bought a few months ago. Loft living did have its advantages. I never dreamed I would ever have an apartment in Manhattan large enough to accommodate my own personal washer and drier.

While the sheets were tumbling dry, a sense of dread began to set in.

No, it wasn't because I feared my whites were going to come out wrinkled.

It was because I knew that in a matter of hours—if I could track him down—I would have to face Detective Joseph Stark again. I might even wind up groveling a little before that arrogant little bastard who had insulted and dismissed me. But I made up my mind that if grovel I had to, then grovel I would.

It was almost enough to inspire me to bake up some poison scones for his coffee break.

Stark was in a slightly better mood this time. At any rate, he kept the sarcasm to a minimum. He was in a great hurry to leave, which was all to the good, I guess. He had no time to toy with me like a kitten with a cockroach.

At the very least, he wasn't ridiculing me anymore. I had the feeling he had done a little checking up on me since our last meeting. Perhaps Rothwax had put in a word for me. But Stark did not mention that, and I did not ask.

He didn't have to check my snapshots against a mug book or any other book, he said. He recognized Brewer "Savannah" Bloodworth at once.

"What are you doing with a loan shark's picture?" he asked me. "Is the detecting business that bad?"

"Loan shark," I repeated. "This man is a brilliant cook who moonlights as a loan shark?"

"Or vice versa," Stark answered. "He

knows his food, anyway. They still miss old Savannah in the kitchen at Dannemora."

"He's done time in Dannemora Prison, you mean?"

"That's right. A couple of terms. And he specializes in lending money to people in the restaurant industry. Likes to hang with that pretentious downtown crowd. And he's got the right line of bullsh—that is, the gift of gab to pull it off. He's pretty slick."

"Yes, Detective. I'd have to agree with that," I said.

"Take some advice," Stark said breezily, pulling a small square brush from his desk drawer and beginning to spiff up his shoes.

"What advice?"

"Walk the other way. Steer clear of him. And if any of your clients are thinking of getting into bed with him—metaphorically, of course—recommend they have their heads shrunk."

"That sounds like sound advice," I said.

"No charge. Now, if you'll excuse me . . . " He let his voice die away as he stood up, a lint brush in his left hand.

My guess was there was a cocktail party at MOMA and Stark's lady friend was waiting for him.

I thanked him hurriedly and left.

I walked home slowly, alone, the evening shadows wrapping me up like a coat.

Every new turn this case took meant a new can of worms.

So Brewer Bloodworth, also known as Savannah, was a criminal. A fairly dangerous one, it sounded like. It was hard to reconcile that with the group he ran with. The pretentious downtown crowd, as Stark had labeled them.

Well, on second thought, perhaps it wasn't so hard to reconcile. After all, one of those people had killed twice.

Bloodworth was a loan shark who specialized in lending to restaurateurs. Another finger pointing to Hector Naciemento, former cafe owner.

My hour with Hector was not far away. As soon as I could figure out how to get to him, get through the protective shield that Grace Ann would certainly have thrown up around her lovely friend.

My little client, the grieving young widow Wiegel, had thrown up her own protective shield around her late husband's life, or so I felt. The day of reckoning between the two of us was going to take place soon also—sooner than she imagined.

I was hungry, but the thought of stopping for a meal alone was completely unappealing. I could have used a nice glass of wine, too. But the last thing I wanted to do was go into a bar alone.

Alone.

*Alone.*

My God. I realized I was feeling lonesome

and sorry for myself. I was acting like some loser in a bad self-help book.

I quickened my step, trying to throw off that lush autumnal wrapping. It was too sappy for words. It was weighing me down. I was mad at autumn.

# Chapter 11

There was a half-empty bottle of Scotch on the coffee table. It was open and the cap was nowhere in sight.

She was drinking. Alone. In the middle of the afternoon. Not good.

Lainie's eyes were moist. I felt awful saying to her the things I had to say to her, but there seemed little choice. She was never going to come clean about Niles and Hector and Brewer Bloodworth on her own. For whatever reason, she still felt the need to protect her husband's reputation. Even in death.

A person dies. Half of us decide that his secrets must die with him, and dedicate our lives to keeping them buried. The other half of us can't wait to air every dirty little secret in the trunk of that person's life.

There were a whole lot of books and plays and films with that theme, weren't there? Like *Citizen Kane*. And there was that pious old Hepburn-Tracy movie, *Keeper of the Flame*. She plays the widow of the beloved, influential American philanthropist and media titan. Tracy is a newspaperman assigned to write the man's epitaph, so to speak, to tell the real story of the revered American hero. Together, the widow and the journalist uncover the truth about the departed—he was a hyperfascist white supremacist with grandiose plans to take over the world—a homegrown American Nazi.

Speaking of grandiose, it was a bit high flown to be comparing Niles Wiegel's life and death to that of the character in that movie. Hepburn's husband had been a nationally known figure of enormous influence; that is why he was potentially so dangerous. Niles Wiegel, on the other hand, had been a nice-looking man in his thirties with good taste in clothes, bad taste in business, and an unfortunate allergy to almonds.

Still, Lainie was covering up for Niles. Protecting him.

Or, who knows? Maybe she wasn't. Maybe she *was* telling me the whole truth. But I didn't believe her. That was the point. It just didn't sound true to me. And so my choice was clear.

"Lainie, I'm afraid I'm going to have to terminate my investigation of Niles's death. I'm ending it, as of now."

"You can't do that!" she wailed.

"Yes, I can, Lainie. I have to."

"But you said you're certain now that

somebody killed Niles. You said Penny's murder convinced you of it."

"Yes. That's true."

Lainie's face reddened with anger. "Then why won't you go on with the investigation?" she shouted. "What kind of game are you playing here? Is it more money you're after? Because I *told* you I can get you money from—"

"Stop it, Lainie! I think you know it isn't the money I'm worried about. And I think you know if anyone is playing games, it isn't me. It's you."

"Me? I don't know what you're talking about."

"Don't you?"

I realized that I was on the verge of losing my temper with her. I didn't want to do that. Tony was under suspicion and clearing him was my first priority. I was going to resign from the investigation no matter what Lainie said. But first I needed to get a few answers from her.

"Listen," I said mildly. "Let's calm down for a moment . . . all right?"

She nodded, picking up her glass.

"All right," I confirmed. "First of all, Lainie, even you must admit how strange it is that you know so little about the man you married. After all, these are the nineties. Young women don't enter arranged marriages anymore, where they have to accept whatever man is chosen for them—no questions asked."

Lainie didn't interrupt me. She sat quietly listening to my monologue.

"From the beginning," I continued, "you've given me next to nothing to go on. You say you don't know how he made his money, you don't know how he could afford to buy the loft, you don't know what the two of you were living on."

She remained wordless.

"Well, Lainie, since you are obviously not a stupid girl, I have to conclude that you have lied to me about Niles. And that your husband Niles—with no visible means of support—was such a good provider because he was doing something underhanded. He was doing something illegal, Lainie. It's only common sense."

With that, she came to life again. Lainie's mouth twisted into a terrible red slash.

"That isn't true!" she shouted. "You shut up about Niles!"

I ignored her outburst. "Did Niles ever mention a man named Brewer Bloodworth? Perhaps he called him 'Savannah.' "

"No."

"No, dear? Are you sure?" I said, being more than a little patronizing.

"You heard my answer, Alice."

"I think you do know that name, Lainie. I think you know that Niles and Hector borrowed money from Mr. Bloodworth, years ago, when they ran the cafe. I think you know that Mr. Bloodworth is a criminal—a loan shark. Was he still bleeding Niles?"

Lainie was suddenly on her feet.

"Get out of here, Alice."

"In a moment I will."

"Not in a moment, lady. Now!"

I forged ahead. "Is Brewer Bloodworth trying to bleed you now, Lainie? Does he know something about Niles and Hector? Did Niles borrow more money from him?"

Lainie was holding the door open, not listening to me. She had my bag and sweater under her arm, waiting for me to pass through the door so that she could hand them to me on the way out.

"You betrayed me, Alice," Lainie said as I stepped into the hallway.

Her martyred look was almost funny. "*I* betrayed *you*? I don't think so, dear. *I* didn't hire an investigator and then lie to her. *I* didn't insist to everyone—including the police—that my husband was murdered, and then proceed to cover up facts that could help solve the murder."

"For the last time," Lainie hissed, "I don't know any Bloodworth. Loan shark or otherwise. For the last time, my husband was a good man who loved and took care of me. And it was Hector Naciemento who killed him."

The grimy old elevator pulled up and its doors squeaked open.

"One last question, Lainie," I said, not expecting to receive an answer.

She turned her sullen face toward me. "What?"

"Did Hector seduce you, too? Is that why you hate him so much?"

The elevator doors closed slowly.

I got him!

It was while I was still trying to figure out how and when I was going to catch up with Hector that I did that very thing.

I was still making periodic calls to Grace Ann and Samantha's brownstone. There was never an answer.

I had stopped in once or twice at that bar on Greene Street that Lainie Wiegel had mentioned—Perfection—just on the off chance that Hector might be having a drink there. But no go.

I had even phoned Sidney Rickover to ask him to intercede. It wouldn't take much, the next time he visited the Collins sisters, to simply give Hector my phone number and ask him to call me. The attorney had agreed to it, if he had a moment alone with Hector. But so far I had heard nothing. And, it was stupid, I realized, to depend on that lovesick lawyer. He had totally forgotten that I wanted to talk to *him*—forget about Hector. No, enlisting the help of a lovelorn middle-aged businessman was probably not my best bet.

Then, on the morning that I was staking out the Collins business address on Forsyth Street, I got him.

Hector left the factory about eleven-thirty and began one of his race walks. He was headed west. He was wearing high-priced jogging sneakers. And so, luckily, was I— even if mine had been a sale item from the clearance table at the shoe store on Eighth Street.

I trailed him across town at a manic clip. And, like before, he ended up at his gym.

I waited twenty minutes or so before going in.

Oh, sure, said the trim young blonde at the reception desk, sure, she knew Mr. Naciemento. He was in the weight room now.

Sitting astride one of those chrome and leather contraptions, Hector smiled graciously at me. As though it was perfectly natural for me to be walking across the hardwood floor toward him. Almost as though he'd been waiting for me to join him for cocktails.

"Alice."

That was all he said. He simply spoke my name. But he managed to suffuse those two syllables with a world of meaning. Some actors I know could learn a lot from this man.

I followed suit. "Hector," I said.

We remained that way for a long moment, him gazing calmly into my eyes, leaning forward on the torture horse, his thin T-shirt slightly moist with perspiration; me standing there, facing him, returning the gaze.

"You know, Hector," I said finally, "I think perhaps we just had sex. But I'm not sure."

He laughed merrily, showing white teeth. "My fault," he said, nodding his apology.

But now, I thought, comes the end of the bliss. No *tristesse* and cigarettes this time, buddy.

I went straight to the heart of the matter. "Hector, how did you and Niles get mixed up with Savannah?"

"With whom?"

"A man named Brewer Bloodworth. Some call him Savannah. He is—or was, at any rate—a loan shark, a dangerous character. Though now he doesn't seem to be doing anything more harmful than blackening red snapper."

Hector went on smiling. "Alice, you are that rare thing, aren't you?"

"Am I? What?"

"A truly witty female. One doesn't often encounter such a woman."

"Well, thank you, Hector."

"Even more rare—you are a very direct female. And so I will not bother to lie to you. Niles and I were very young, and very naive about . . . business. We had no idea what we were getting ourselves into with a restaurant. We thought having a place where stylish, influential people gathered would be fun. And it was, I assure you. But it wasn't long before we were in over our heads. Mr. Bloodworth came to our rescue—even if it wasn't merely out of the goodness of his heart. He is no altruist, that's for sure. It was a struggle to get out from under his demands, but we finally did it. We lost the cafe in the end, along with our innocence. And we moved on with our lives. There—is that what you wanted to know?"

"It's a start."

Hector laughed again. "Very well. Go on. What else would you like to know?"

"I've been told you and Niles were not on good terms before his death. Is there any truth to that?"

"Some."

"What was the trouble between you?"

"Ah. There, I'm afraid my candor will have to stop. It was a purely personal matter. The kind of thing I would never discuss with a lady."

"Not even Grace Ann?"

"No. Not even Grace Ann."

"Are you positive, Hector? Couldn't it have been something she could help you with—monetarily at least."

I had insulted him. But not even that fazed him.

"Money solves so many problems," he said evenly. "But not this one."

"No," I said. "No, I suppose you're right. It wouldn't help if, for instance, you'd been having an affair with Lainie Wiegel and Niles found out about it."

He seemed genuinely surprised—and hurt—by that remark. He made no reply, however.

Damn, he was good. I was beginning to feel like a dirty-minded little gossip. Some people were masters at turning the tables. Hector might have been an evil character, but he knew how to handle people.

I had to return to my former bluntness before he finessed me right out of the room. "You can remain silent if you like, Hector, but I know you were sleeping with Penny Motion."

"Oh yes," he said quietly. "That was an indiscretion I have come to truly regret."

"Did Grace Ann know about it before Penny was murdered?"

"No, of course not. Grace Ann is my kindest friend. I would never have—"

"Did you take money from her to help Penny out?"

"We were lovers, Penny and I. Lovers help each other out, as you say, in any number of ways."

"Did you kill Penny?"

I saw anger flash in and out of his dreamy eyes then. He said simply, "No."

"Did you love her?"

"Again, Alice, some matters must remain personal. I will say only that it is possible to love more than one woman at one time.

You're a beautiful woman. Have you never found yourself in similar circumstances?"

I chose not to go down that road. I ignored the question. "Hector," I said confidingly, "I'm sure you know by now some people think Niles's death was no accident."

"You number yourself among them, no doubt."

"Correct."

"And you wish to know whether I agree?"

"Nope. I wish to know whether you killed him. You did, didn't you?"

He had regained all his composure by then. Hector lifted himself effortlessly off the exercise machine and slid an immaculate white towel around his neck. "Perhaps you'd like to hear my answer in the pool."

"Excuse me?"

"I'm inviting you for a swim, Alice."

"Some other time."

"I wish you meant that," he said, stepping very close to me.

There was that look again. That way he had of drawing you near with those eyes.

Hector placed his hand on my shoulder. I looked down at the baby blanket of fine dark hairs that started at his wrist and ran up his bronzed forearm.

I came up with a sentence I thought would be effective—and there wasn't an ounce of wit in it. But before I could speak, he kissed me.

Kissed me! Yes.

And as he did it—his full, firm mouth on mine—he applied a steady, soft pressure at the small of my back—and I caught that anomalously sweet wave of male sweat—and for just a second my knees seemed to buckle.

I knew exactly how corny the gesture was, but when at last he released me, I slapped the living hell out of him.

Not even that removed the smile from his lips. Instead, he shook his head regretfully. "I must be going now, Alice. Pity. I predicted great things for us."

"You killed them!" I called after him.

But Hector was gone.

Fliss laughed so hard that he needed a tissue to dry his tears.

"My Lord, Alice. Your life is better than an episode of *Melrose Place*. Still waters, my darling, still waters."

I took another fat gingersnap from the blue china plate. I had arrived in the middle of his teatime.

"I'm glad you think it's so amusing," I told him.

"Oh my, yes. You're joining a very long queue, dear. Hector's conquests are limitless."

"Don't count me as one of his conquests, Fliss. In fact, he may be my conquest. I just might nail him for two murders."

"Do you seriously think he could have done it?"

"You'd be surprised at who is capable of murder, Fliss. And why. Obviously, they're not all gangsters, not always hardened criminals. Which brings me to another point, actually. Something I need to ask you."

*"Moi?"*

"Yes. It's about Brewer Bloodworth. Also known as Savannah."

"Of all the boring *noms de plume*! Couldn't he have come up with something a tad more imaginative?"

"Maybe it wasn't his choice," I said.

"So true. Perhaps the other inmates at that darling prison facility bestowed it upon him."

"Perhaps. But, what I'm wondering is, how could you—and all the other people in the fashion industry—have known Bloodworth—used his catering services—partied with him and so on—and not have a hint that he was a loan shark—a gangster?"

Fliss sighed. "Slow learner, aren't you, Alice? Don't you know that, with the possible exception of Lady Di, no one in that world is who he claims to be?"

"No one?"

"Absolutely no one."

"Does that include you, Fliss?"

He roared with laughter. "Especially me, you silly cow. Didn't I tell you—when I was a fair-haired lad watching the Late Show, the movie *Laura* changed my life. Clifton Webb as Waldo Lydecker became my ideal, Alice. My Idol. But I'm no Waldo. What I really am is one of those poor creatures from *The Wizard of Oz*."

"You mean like the Scarecrow?"

"*Precise*, precious. I'm self-invented, sweetie. All sawdust and feathers and smoke. But does that mean I'm not just as fabulous as the next ninny?"

I smiled and shrugged.

"Now, pass me that sherry and quit stuffing your gob with sweets."

I felt terribly confused. And a little tight. I'd had three sherries in Fliss's rooms.

I was wandering aimlessly along 23rd Street. In a kind of fog. Hoping I wouldn't walk into any brick walls. It was like this crazy investigation. Nothing added up, exactly. The clues, the people, the secrets all swirled around me, clouding everything. And there were so many brick walls.

How had Tony put it that day? He said he'd make a "bold move." That was it. It seemed ten years ago that he made that remark. It was when he lied to me about encountering Penny Motion in a midtown bar and taking the opportunity to go through her purse.

A bold move was certainly called for now. But I didn't have one.

I had made it all the way to Third Avenue. I was less than five minutes away from my old apartment, where Basillio was now living. It must have been all the thinking about him that drew me over this way.

I stopped at a deli and bought some sandwiches and juice and coffee. You couldn't count on Basillio to have anything more than a bulb of garlic and a quart of some gooey ice cream in the refrigerator.

I still had the keys. I let myself into the lobby door, stopping briefly to look fondly at my old mailbox. Then I began the long climb up.

I knocked several times before I heard sounds of movement from within. Then, at last, I heard the locks being turned. The door opened wide.

I nearly dropped the grocery bag when Tony appeared in the doorway. He looked horrible!

He was still in his bathrobe, beneath it a crumpled T-shirt and old pajama bottoms. Unshaven. Bare feet. Hair wild. He had lost almost ten pounds.

"My God, Tony, what's the matter with you?"

He shrugged listlessly.

I set the groceries down and rushed over to him. I felt his forehead with the palm of my hand, at the same time using my foot to slam the door shut.

I knew I could count on Mrs. Oshrin. And she came through. She had numberless cans of soup in the cabinet, and she brought over a selection of them. I got Tony back into bed and force-fed him hot chicken broth.

Basillio's fever was negligible. So what *was* the matter with him?

In my opinion he had the unnameable malady. It was the kind of thing anybody anywhere could come down with, I suppose. But I've always considered it an illness unique to city dwellers—part flu, part over-work, part heartbreak, and, overshadowing everything, part depression. How many of us have spent day after paralyzed day on our sofas eating too much or too little, watching soap operas or staring at the ceiling, crying incessantly or numb with sadness. In time, it passes. If we're lucky, there's someone with soup and sympathy to ring the buzzer and help us get through to the other side of it.

Tony had it bad.

I began to talk to him about the dead ends and the frustrations of the case. Eventually, he began to respond.

Within a couple of hours he had eaten both the sandwiches and was throwing out his own theories about who was guilty and who wasn't.

Along the way we had to open up the

painful wound of his short-lived affair with Penny Motion. That was a difficult one. Personally, I didn't want to hear about the affair. But as an investigator, I *had* to hear it—had to listen and take in every detail and probe and ask for more.

While he spoke, he pretended not to cry and I pretended not to notice his tears.

One thing we agreed on. Penny, in death, maybe even more than in life, might be the key to breaking open the case.

Basillio even put together our next bold move: we had to get into that 14th Street office—or factory or workroom—whatever it was—where Penny Motion's mysterious design firm was headquartered. I still had the address on the slip of paper Tony had given me.

There was only one thing we disagreed on. One sticking point. *We* had to get into the office, Tony said. *We*.

There could be no "we" for this job. Tony was in enough trouble. As a suspect in Penny's murder, the last thing in the world he needed was to be caught breaking into her place—a place the authorities might not even know exists.

Besides, Tony still had that malady. I knew all the stages of it. He might be talking animatedly with me now. But I was going to leave him soon, and he knew it. And he knew I hadn't forgiven him yet. No, the sickness was still with him. He wouldn't be on his feet—ready for adventure like this one—for another day or two.

And so I was going to embark on a new career, as a second-story specialist.

And that was a one-woman show. A solo.

# Chapter 12

Luckily, someone was there to talk me out of my foolish plan to go wandering around alone in the so-called meat district in the middle of the night, with the intention to commit the very serious crime of breaking and entering.

Who was the voice of sanity? Alison, my niece.

She talked sense and I listened. But actually—even though I accepted what she said—my plan wouldn't have to change at all, except in one regard: I wouldn't be wandering alone.

Alison was coming with me.

And so was Felix, her kindhearted, mild-mannered, slightly balding, scholarly psychiatrist boyfriend, also my landlord.

I didn't see anything so difficult in this legendary breaking and entering. Basically, I'd have to describe it as a snap. People like me, having been brought up on a dairy farm, learn to "break and enter" at a young age. You have to. Barn doors are always warping or freezing shut. Windows are constantly jamming. Nature seems to conspire to keep you locked out or locked in. So you learn the art of forced entry very quickly.

We were inside in a matter of seconds.

Felix went in ahead of us, to check things out. He shone his discreet hi-tech flashlight into this corner and that, and then came back to the door to motion us in.

It was only when we'd closed all the blinds and turned on the table lamp that I got a good look at Alison's outfit. She was the perfect little cat burglar in the perfect little black cat suit. I'd seen it in the window of Boutique Ariel last month.

Amusingly enough, Felix was dressed to match Alison's getup. He had on black jeans and black turtleneck and a buttery black leather jacket—with only two or three tasteful zippers running hither and thither across his chest.

But no Batman-type masks for them. Thank God.

Asked by my two assistants for instructions on what they should look for, I told them "Anything."

We wanted letters, receipts, bank statements, canceled checks—anything.

We found none of those things.

Indeed, aside from the rack of clothing at the rear of the studio, two cutting tables, the sewing machine, and a few packets of instant coffee, there was nothing to find in the studio. What it looked like was a place that had recently been stripped clean. Carefully, methodically stripped. Like a dog strips sinews from a bone. My hunch was that someone from our circle of fashion-world suspects had been here before us.

I told Alison and Felix that there seemed to be nothing more for us to do here. "It's not as if we brought along a fingerprint dusting kit or anything," I joked.

"You know, I can get you one of those, Alice," Felix called to me over one shoulder as he walked toward the lone rack of clothing.

"Thanks very much, Felix. I'll let you know."

Alison and I joined him at the rear of the studio.

My niece lifted up one of the garments on its hanger and then immediately pushed it away from her. "Well, Auntie Alice. If these are Penny's creations, I think Monsieur Givenchy can sleep well tonight."

She sauntered back across the room and checked her seams in the full-length mirror.

The "creations" Alison referred to were pretty dreadful. Jackets and vests made of washed denim—and in some cases *not* washed—deliberately, if not artfully, torn or shredded in various spots. Sewn onto the garments were patches of stained lace and tiny religious icons and political slogans from times gone by.

However, some of the garments had the loveliest buttons I had ever seen.

Being a farm girl at heart, I dearly love buttons. I leaned in closer to try to discern the pattern on one of the intricately carved buttons. I looked over to see that Felix was even more engrossed in the same activity.

"Did you *see* these?" he asked in amazement.

"They're really lovely, aren't they?"

"They're a whole lot more than that, Alice. These are remarkable! They're genuine whalebone, you know. And look at the detail work. Truly remarkable! I'd have to look him up when I get home, but I think I might know who the artist was who worked on these."

"Felix knows everything, Aunt Alice," my niece called from across the room. "Ask him any question about Early American quilts, Navajo beadwork, art deco pottery, German fountain pens . . . oh, the list is endless. But unfortunately, Felix doesn't just talk about those things—he owns them—or, rather, *collects* them. And soon . . . " she flew to Felix's side and kissed him on the cheek " . . . soon I'll have to move out of the house to make room for his—what is it?—whalebone button collection."

"No you won't, my love," Felix said cheerfully. "I'll just buy you a bigger house."

"Nice Felix," my niece said, rubbing his head.

*Nice Felix,* I echoed the thought silently. It was unbelievable to me now that I'd once thought of him as a scoundrel of the worst sort.

We flicked off the lamp and prepared to leave. Then I turned around and went back over to the rack of denim vests and jackets.

We'd come here to break the law, but so far, except for some mild "b & e," we hadn't done a thing wrong.

So I decided it was high time I stole something.

Just off the Hudson River, the meat district, as that little enclave far west on 14th Street is known, can be a pretty frightening place at night. It's dark as death and the collection of characters roaming around spans the gamut from brave tourists searching for out-of-the-way steak houses, to drunk college kids reeling out of the Irish pub, to purse snatchers, to overaggressive transvestite hookers.

And the rats reign supreme! Alison and I held on to Felix as we walked, saying nothing, listening to the scrabbling and rustling emanating from the gauntlet of black Hefty bags in the gutter. Here and there lay actual meat scraps, stray gristle and bone, the detritus from the nearby commercial butchers.

The neighborhood didn't seem to trouble Felix very much. He looked like a man out for a pleasant evening stroll, who just happened to have a stricken blond woman on each arm.

"I'm ravenous!" Felix said when we reached the more familiar terrain of Christopher Street. "Anybody else hungry?"

Alison and I exchanged glances, each seeming to wait for the other's answer. Finally, we both nodded at Felix.

On the way back to Felix's Barrow Street brownstone, we stopped at a gourmet deli and went wild in the aisles. We amassed enough food to feed the entire Village.

With the denim vest I'd taken from Penny's loft under my arm, I stopped on 6th Avenue long enough to call Tony.

"How are you, Basillio? Feeling any better?" I asked when he picked up the phone.

He made a noncommittal sound in answer. "Did you find anything at Penny's business office?"

"Precious little. I think the rats got there first."

"What rats?"

"Never mind. Are you feeling strong enough to get into a taxi and come to Felix's place?"

"Why?"

"A sophisticated food blowout. I found some Provolone you'll love. And Felix says he's got a bottle of red wine with your name on it."

"Well," Tony began, "I'm not sure I ought—"

" 'Course you should, *paisan*! We got sweet for you, we got sour. We got roast pork, we got candy. Everything but your old Aunt Emily's cherry pie. So come on down! It'll do you good to get out of the house."

He was at the door in fifteen minutes.

We stuffed ourselves on Black Forest ham and white asparagus and sour dough bread baked with olives and imported cheeses and stuffed grape leaves and out-of-season yellow cherries and hand-dipped bittersweet chocolates and everything else in the garden.

Suddenly Alison dropped a stuffed grape leaf onto the floor. It had squirted out of her fingers like a fish.

"Wait!" she yelled out.

We all stopped eating and stared at her. She, in turn, was staring at the fallen grape leaf. Something was disturbing her, obviously.

"What's the matter, love?" asked a dutiful and always concerned Felix.

On the edge of some kind of hysteria, she responded: "Why are we all eating like this? What are we doing? Why are we celebrating?"

"Excitement," Felix responded. "The excitement made us hungry."

"What excitement? All we did is push open a creaky door in a dead woman's shop," she said.

Alison glared at us all.

Then she looked at herself—at her cat burglar outfit. "And I am ridiculous for dressing like this. Just totally ridiculous." She gave me a special accusatory look. No one knew how to respond to her. Perhaps she had a point.

Felix used a napkin to pick up the fallen food.

"We did what we had to do," I said.

"No, Aunt Alice. You did what you have to do. I love you very much but you have this infuriating ability to implicate everyone in your adventures. And it always ends up that you look wise and we look stupid."

"No one here appears stupid to me. I am thankful for your help."

Alison sat back down and began to chew on a piece of bread. She was still agitated but trying to control herself. Felix looked confused. Tony looked away.

I wanted very much to put my arms around my niece but I didn't. I felt on the verge of tears. But I had the feeling that this strange outburst wasn't about anything that had happened during the past hours or days. Or even anything that had happened since she had come back to the U.S. from France. It was something about her dead husband . . . the young man who killed himself in France. It was something about the outfit she was wearing and the break-in that had transported her back to another time and place. She had rarely spoken about those times to me. Perhaps not to Felix, either. "Would you like to hear some music?" Felix asked of no one in particular.

"That would be nice," I said.

"That would be nice," Alison said and I had the feeling that she was making fun of me . . . mocking me with the exact same words and inflection.

"As long as it isn't 'Death and the Maiden,' " Tony said wryly.

Suddenly everyone burst out laughing. And a few seconds later Alison's hysteria was history and we had returned to our stomachs.

We had coffee and brandy in the library. Tony and Alison—I don't think she'd ever eaten that much in her life—shared the sofa, laid out like corpses. Felix was poring over one of his oversize reference books.

I excused myself for a moment and went into the hallway. When I returned I was wearing the denim vest I'd taken from Penny's office.

"Oh no," Alison groaned. "Please take that thing away! The sight of that filthy garment makes me sick."

"Sorry, dear," I said. "I just thought it might provide some tender nostalgia for Tony here." And I did a little imitation of that inanely spirited swishy walk that fashion models affect on the runway.

Tony sat up. "What are you talking about?"

"I believe this is the handiwork of the late Ms. Motion. I wondered if this kind of thing was among the many talents she revealed to you . . . .Recognize it?"

Silence.

Alison's face went cherry red.

Finally, Tony spoke. "That was low, Swede—I mean, Alice. Even if you have due cause to be nasty to me."

A pall fell over the room. I knew that I had gone too far.

Why had I taken the jacket?

Stolen it, rather. I had stolen it. It wasn't my property. Even worse—I had stolen it from the dead.

Since when was Alice Nestleton a thief? The last object I had stolen was a long time ago. At age thirteen to be exact. And the object was a beautiful Mont Blanc fountain pen.

I stole it from Sue Dranger, who sat next to me in homeroom.

The theft was quickly detected and I was sent to the principal's office. Then I was sent home.

When I arrived, a phone call to my grandmother had already been made by the principal.

"Why did you do that?" Gram asked me.

I remember that we were in the huge kitchen. She was cleaning one of her pots, scraping every last bit of residue from it.

I didn't answer. She wiped her hands on a towel.

"Did you hear me, Alice?"

And then I gave her a smart-alecky answer. Something like . . . well . . . I had this bottle of ink and I didn't know what to do with it, so rather than throw it away I figured I would steal a pen.

Yes, it was very smark alecky, but that's what thirteen-year-old girls are about.

She slapped me right in the face.

And then we stared at each other in horror.

Then we both burst into tears.

That was the last thing I ever stole. Until now.

Why had I taken the jacket? At the moment I did it, I really had no reason. I just did it.

It wasn't my style, that's for sure. Or even my size. It was a little tight on me.

I closed my eyes for a moment. I felt shame. The reality was there. I had stolen it to mock Tony's affection for the young woman. Oh yes, that was it. To make fun of his affection for a punk girl. Elegant Alice Nestleton would never wear anything like it. I had stolen it to make a vindictive present to him.

I had to face facts. It was the act of a jealous, vindictive, vengeful woman. I was paying Tony back.

But I had to continue the charade in a modified form. At least in front of Alison and Felix.

"I'm very sorry, Tony. That was . . . disrespectful . . . to Penny and to you. I shouldn't have said it that way. But, do you recognize it?"

He shook his head.

I slipped the vest off.

"Let me see that again, Alice," Felix called over to me.

Together we examined one of the luminescent buttons under Felix's magnifier. The design on this one was a beautifully worked harpoon—a typical New England motif, as Felix put it. He made periodic comparisons to some other buttons pictured in his reference book.

"Well," he said at last, "I can't say positively whose work these are, but there's no doubt they're heirlooms. Genuine whalebone from the 1840s. One of these buttons is worth the price of ten of these little jackets—or whatever they are. Being so small and portable, things like buttons and fountain pens and so on get stolen a lot. There's a pretty brisk trade in hot collectibles such as these. Particularly if it was carved in New Bedford.

"But I think Miss Motion simply didn't know how to—what's the word?—'fence' something like this. And of course there's the possibility she didn't realize their value at all. So she wound up using them on her—"

"Creations," I supplied.

"Yes," he affirmed, starting after Alison as she wobbled out of the room.

She had eaten herself sick. I sympathized. But my mind was elsewhere. On robbery. Highway and otherwise.

The whole evening had its roots in robbery, I realized.

And that was what this case might be all about, too!

Yes, the whole strange, murky mess of paté death might well be about perfectly coherent larceny.

It took my breath away. Particularly since only my own meanspiritedness in stealing the jacket had made that coherence possible.

# Chapter 13

Detective Stark was not happy to see me. To be truthful, that came as no surprise.

Once again I had interrupted his breakfast. I guess he was figuring on a slow day, because piled neatly beside his cappuccino were all four daily New York newspapers. He was just beginning the perusal when I knocked softly at the half-opened door and pushed in to the room.

He didn't really groan audibly. But his unhappiness was there on his face.

Nor did he remonstrate immediately at my visit. What he did do was to fix his stare at a point on the far wall.

"I won't take up a lot of your time," I said, settling into the chair across from his desk. "I promise."

He heaved an enormous sigh, brought his eyes back to the newspapers, and said quietly: "Yes. And the check is in the mail—right?"

"Excuse me?"

"It doesn't matter. For some reason there

are a lot of clichéd phrases in my head at the moment. Some of them downright filthy."

I smiled. So this was the way it was going to be.

"Detective Stark, I think I owe you an apology for ever thinking of you as the new breed of police officer."

"By the way," Stark said, "how many times have you been here to see me? Five? Six?"

"No. Not that many. I believe this is the third time I've spoken to you."

"Really? Somehow I thought it was many more. In fact I was thinking that since you seem to love this precinct house so much—I mean, you've logged an impressive number of hours here—I thought maybe you might like to join our police auxiliary. They give you a rather attractive, conservative blue uniform and a nice badge—and then of course it goes without saying that we could see each other every day."

There was something so completely familiar about this kind of animosity that at first I couldn't place it. It really didn't make me angry; almost kind of wistful. Then I realized why. Stark sounded like one of those boy genius directors I used to deal with. Their speech was a constant stream of low-level abuse of others.

All I said in response was, "Blue is not my color."

Then I dropped one of the buttons on the desk in front of him. It made too loud a sound, as if I were throwing it down in anger.

He sat back and stared at it. Then he leaned forward once again, until his face was no more than three inches from the button. He was regarding it as if it were a miniature spaceship.

But, after a minute, when no little green men emerged, he took a sip from his cup, ruffled the pages of one of the newspapers, and asked: "What is that?"

"A button," I replied.

"I don't sew."

"If you don't sew, Detective, you'll never reap."

"Ah hah. You also did vaudeville?"

"It's a nineteenth-century whalebone button, beautifully carved, as you can see."

"How splendid," he said, nodding his appreciation.

"And it's part of an antique button collection that was stolen."

"You don't say?"

"Can you trace it for me? Can you tell me where and when the collection was stolen? And from whom? Surely there must be insurance reports and police reports in your files."

He stared at the button and asked with sublime mockery: "Is this valuable piece of evidence important to that *dreadful* paté murder case?"

"Yes. And to another *dreadful* murder that is now being investigated by Manhattan North."

"Do you want me to put the entire squad on this button? How about some SWAT teams? Internal Affairs also? Or do you want me to set up a joint federal-state task force?"

"I need your help, Detective. It's important."

He picked up the button and rattled it, as if he were throwing dice.

"Now you listen to me, Miss Nestleton, or Madame Nestleton—or is it simply Alice in Wonderland? No. The answer is no. I will not lift one finger to trace this button for you. But how nice it was to get another visit from you. I look forward to seeing you again." With that, he reached across the desk and dropped the button into my hand.'

I left the station house and walked ten blocks north in a smoldering rage before I regained some kind of control. Then I knew I had to call Rothwax. He was the only one who could help me now.

It took me four quarters to find a working street phone and get the number of the Korean Merchants Association. Finally I was connected to the director of security. Rothwax's voice was a balm.

"I need an important favor," I said.

"You always did," he replied, laughing. There was silence. Then he seemed to sense my angst. He said: "Look, I have to be at a Korean greengrocer on Seventeenth and Park this afternoon about two. They've been having trouble with kids from the local high school. Why don't you meet me there at about two-thirty. Then you can tell me your troubles. Okay?"

"That would be fine."

He said, "By the way, how is your friend doing?"

At first I didn't know which friend he meant. I had forgotten that it was Rothwax who called me that night to say the police were questioning Tony about poor Penny's murder. He had called me in the middle of the night.

"Tony is fine," I lied.

"Good. See ya at two," he said and hung up.

I had several hours to kill but I didn't go back to my loft. I spent most of them in an enormous new bookstore on 6th Avenue with a coffee shop inside the store. I leafed through dozens of magnificently illustrated cat books. Then I moved to books about old movies. Then I graduated to exotic cookbooks. After cookbooks, including a delicious one that recreated the greatest recipes from none other than Marcel Proust's table, I went to practical guidebooks for the aspiring young actor. These afforded me a great deal of wry humor, to say the least.

Then, thoroughly agitated, I walked to

17th and Park. Rothwax was waiting for me, very much the corporate officer, with attaché case. I wondered if he had an instructional manual in it, in Korean and English, that taught clerks how to deal with kids who steal apples.

He looked very much the same . . . well, a bit more portly, and his red hair had thinned even more. As usual, his big hands looked newly manicured. He still wore a suit twenty years out of date and highly polished shoes. His tie was a bad dream.

"Long time," he said. We shook hands. "You look awful good, Cat Woman," he added.

We went to the Old Town Bar on 18th Street and sat in a booth. I ordered a ginger ale. Rothwax ordered a bottle of dark beer. We decided to share a grilled cheese and tomato sandwich. American cheese, Rothwax preferred.

"Do you miss the NYPD?" I asked.

"On Tuesdays and Thursdays," he replied.

Enough small talk. I put the button on the table. I told him what it was. I told him what I needed to know.

And then he did a wonderful thing. He picked up the button, placed it in a napkin, carefully rolled it up and put the package into the handkerchief pocket of his suit. Somehow, the gesture inspired tremendous confidence.

"I'll do what I can, Cat Woman. But remember, I don't have access to the computer anymore. Or files. I'll just make some calls and see what I can dig up."

"Thank you," I said.

"Things getting you down?"

"Do I look it?"

"You look tired."

"I am that . . . and frightened."

"Aren't we all?" noted Rothwax.

The sandwich arrived. We each took half.

"Will you be home tonight?" he asked.

"Yes."

"I'll get back to you sometime this evening."

"If I step out . . . just put it on the machine."

He nodded. Then said: "How about a brandy?"

"No, thanks."

"Mind if I have one?"

I smiled, reached across the table, and patted his hand in that way very old folks have with that particular gesture. I *am* getting old, I thought.

We sat at home waiting for the call—Bushy and Pancho and I.

Oh, Tony was there, too, but things between us continued to be tense, so we were keeping our distance from each other—each giving the other space, as the expression went.

For some reason, that evening, I took out

my portfolio of clippings, which had never been assiduously maintained. I looked through several of the reviews of plays and my performances in them. The best were still the reviews of my Shakespearian roles at the Guthrie Theater in Minneapolis—before I came to New York. One of the reviewers said he would bet the barn that I would become one of the great ladies of the American theater. I must have impressed him. Obviously, he had already lost the barn. There were no reviews of my cat-sitting skills, although in that area I was sure I had become the grand dame of New York City cat-sitting. That was probably why my business had dried up—cat people were too awed by my reputation to ask for rates.

At precisely ten-forty, the phone rang.

Once. Twice. It was harsh. My cats pricked up their ears.

"Well, pick it up!" Tony said.

"No!"

I don't know why I didn't pick up the phone. Maybe I was afraid Rothwax wouldn't have found out anything. Maybe I wanted it all on tape.

Anyway, after four rings the machine kicked in. I heard my own voice. Then I listened to Rothwax's message.

God bless Detective Rothwax. It was one of the longest telephone messages I had ever received. Almost seven minutes. And he, as they say, had brought home the bacon.

"Play it, Tony," I said after Rothwax hung up.

"Play it again, Tony," I said.

I listened to it six times. And it rang at least as many bells.

What he found out was this:

The button I gave him was part of a collection stolen, along with rare coins and porcelain, from a posh Central Park building about eight months ago.

There had been several such robberies of high-security buildings on Central Park West and Central Park South over a three-year period.

The robberies stopped as suddenly as they started.

The thieves were never identified and never caught.

Having an uncanny knack for knowing when the apartment owners were away, they had all the time in the world once they entered the place. And they were thorough—they took what they wanted of the heavily insured items, and left without a trace.

They were a team, but no one knows how many thieves were involved.

In one break-in, there was a guard dog in the apartment. They gave the dog drugged chopped sirloin. The dog, alas, was allergic to the sedative, and died.

In another instance, an old woman with a bad heart was in one of the apartments that was being burglarized, suffered a seizure, and died.

But since these two events were obviously accidental and incidental to the team's M.O., the cops have not charged them with other than breaking and entering and grand larceny.

The cops dubbed the bandits "Show White and the Seven Dwarfs" because they were fast, clean, and nonviolent.

That essentially was what Detective Rothwax told my phone machine. He also apologized for not being able to obtain for me the name and address of the owner of the collection. And he closed with: "Good hunting, Cat Woman."

I must have paced for an hour after that phone call. All my synapses were firing.

Tony kept saying "Slow down."

Pancho and I kept passing each other.

"I don't understand why you're getting so worked up," Tony said. "Your friend's phone call didn't mean anything to me. I mean, you knew the button was probably part of a collection. Button . . . button . . . who's got the stupid button? Where did it come from? Who gives a damn!"

"I give a damn."

"Why? It was stolen."

"I care who owned the button and who stole it."

"Rothwax obviously can't help you there."

"I can do it myself," I said. And I gestured that he should be quiet.

I went to the refrigerator and took out half a bar of bittersweet chocolate. I ate it. The jangling in my head had calmed down. I was focused. I knew what I had to do next.

"We're going over to Felix and Alison's," I announced.

"Now? It's past midnight."

"What a nice hour for a visit," I replied.

"But what for?"

"To read a few magazines."

"Wonderful!" Tony exclaimed, as if the world had gone mad.


Felix opened the door of his Barrow Street brownstone for us.

"Is it an emergency?" he asked anxiously, as if only emergencies could explain such an unannounced visit at that time of night.

"Your bathrobe is lovely, Felix," I noted and walked past him into the hallway and then into what used to be called a parlor— where my niece was watching an old Raf Vallone gangster movie on the VCR.

"Did you bring popcorn?" she asked.

"Alison, do you still subscribe to *Vogue*?"

"Of course, Aunt Alice. No self-respecting supermodel would be caught dead without the current issue."

"Well, dear, it isn't the current issue I'm after. It's the back issues."

"How far back?"

"As far back as you have, Alison."

She shrugged. "We try, Felix and me, but we don't do very well with our recycling. So there's always a mountain of paper and magazines. I've got lots of old *W*'s and *Harper's Bazaar*'s, too, and . . . I forget what others."

"Where do you keep them?" I asked. Tony rolled his eyes as if it were inconceivable that we would barge in on people after midnight in order to read fashion magazines.

"In the kitchen, near the back door," she replied.

"Sit down, Tony. Relax. Watch the movie." Tony sat down gingerly. Felix waved to us as he climbed the stairs to go to bed.

I walked into the kitchen and saw the magazines stacked precariously on a small folding table right next to the garbage pail.

I waded into them, almost with a fury. I didn't know who I was looking for but I did know what I was looking for.

It was two hours later when I walked back into the parlor.

Alison was fast asleep on the sofa.

Tony was partially awake, squinting at some kind of foreign language news on TV.

"How did it go?" he croaked.

"Fine. We're about to catch a murderer."

"Can't it wait until morning?"

"There's no rush, Tony. Unless you're squeamish about dead bodies . . . the way I am."

Then, suddenly, I felt affectionate toward Tony. I let my hand go through his hair. Tony perked up. The faintest promise of love always got his attention.

"Tell me, Tony. Do you think it would be proper to have Felix host a soiree on Sunday night to thank all the people who are making Alison and me into world-class models?"

"It's kind of short notice."

"That's for sure."

"Will the murderer be there?"

"As sure as God made little green apples, Tony."

"Is the murderer going to confess before or after coffee?"

"After he sees that denim jacket with the whalebone buttons. And he's really going to confess. He's going to attempt to kill the one wearing it."

"And who might that be?" Tony asked.

"Me."

# Chapter 14

Sunday was a good day for a party, someone had told me recently. Whoever it was
also said that Manhattan people go out on
the town on Thursday night the way they
once did on Saturday night. What do they
do on Saturday night? I asked. They have
people over, I was told.

There was a very nice turnout for Felix
and Alison's party—secretly *my* party, since
I'd put them up to hosting it. The entire cast
of characters was on board—the Collinses
along with their assistant, Julia, and
Samantha's admirer, Sidney Rickover, Hector, Lainie Wiegel, Brewer Bloodworth, who
had the night off because the restaurant
was closed on Sunday, all the models from
the last shoot in my loft, Fliss, Hedy, and at
least a dozen people I didn't recognize.

Fliss and Hedy, no doubt, were responsible for all the uncommonly beautiful people
who were drinking like fish and laying waste
to the food. They all seemed ravenous.

Felix had outdone himself. The fastidiously "correct" caterer had provided more than twenty types of hot and cold canapés and almost that many cheeses. And a staff of wispy young people in white aprons were seeing to it that no glass remained empty for longer than a breath.

I was wearing the denim jacket with the whalebone buttons, circulating with champagne glass in hand. I know I looked rather dumb with that denim oddity over my nice black dress, but understated elegance wasn't the point today.

The Collins sisters each smiled and waved at me, as did the lovesick lawyer in Samantha's wake. I could tell that Grace Ann was laughing at my vest.

I had my niece's bone structure to thank for this evening. I couldn't help but think that this crowd would never have turned out at my invitation. No. It was Alison's youth and great looks—and the speculation that she would soon be famous—that brought them here tonight. Besides, three-quarters of the suspects were mad at me.

I saw Hector greet the New Orleans chef and loan shark. I'd seen warmer exchanges during a fistfight. They must have been the only two people in the room who did not kiss each other in greeting.

Lord, I thought folks in the theater were bad enough. I'd seen enough smooching and hugging tonight to last the rest of my life.

Across the room I spotted Lainie, Niles's

widow. She looked smashing in a bright red dress with a diamond brooch shaped like a horse's head. She was flirting severely with a young man I did not know. He was one of the few men who looked exactly right with a three-day growth of beard. I had to force myself to stop staring at his chin.

So, I suppose it was a fairly happy party.

Only Tony was morose. He hung back, along the walls, as if searching for shadows to hide in. I knew what was going on in his head. He couldn't accept the fact that Penny Motion's friends had already forgotten her. They had forgotten the live Penny. And they had forgotten the dead Penny. But Tony didn't understand. That was what the fashion world lived off—forgetting. And then remembering.

Someone produced the proof sheets from the shoot in my loft and they were handed around with oohs and ahs.

I caught a glimpse of myself and felt like a fool.

Suddenly someone whispered in my ear from behind: "Are you sure she's here?"

I turned. It was Tony.

"Who are you talking about?"

"The murderer."

"How do you know it's a she?"

He gestured for me to come back with him along the wall. I did so. "I don't know for sure it's a she. I don't know anything because you don't tell me anything," he said bitterly.

"You just do what you're supposed to do," I warned him. He glared at me. Then his face softened and he played with one of the buttons on my jacket.

"Scrumptious bait, you are, Swede," he said.

"That's Alice to you, Tony. Not Swede. Remember?" I didn't wait for his confirmation, though. "It's nine-thirty, Tony. Only ninety minutes left."

"Do we have to synchronize watches? What is this commando routine you're doing?"

"Get yourself something to eat," I said and wandered off.

I continued to circulate, flaunting my bad taste.

Hector approached me, that vapidly seductive smile on his lips.

"Ah, look who's here . . . it's beautiful Alice! Hello. Your ensemble is quite interesting, Alice . . . quite adventuresome. May I say that you look lovely tonight?

"Who could prevent you, Hector?" I responded, doing my own version of a simper. I suppose I was still angry at him for that stolen kiss at the gym. But, at the same time, Hector induced in me the wish to be Groucho Marx. And Harpo, too. I'd give a lot to see smooth, sexy Hector's face when I pulled out my red fright wig and blew my bicycle horn in his face.

"I understand that you have met my old friend Brewer," Hector continued.

"Yes," I said, "I have. Although I don't recall his using the word friend when he mentioned your name. You and Niles had a bad falling-out with Mr. Bloodworth, didn't you?"

"Did we? It all seems so long ago. I'm a great believer in letting go of the past and living very much in the present."

"Good for you, Hector," I said mischievously. "I suppose that means that your friend Niles is only a memory for you now."

"I wouldn't say that. Not yet."

"And what about his wife? Lainie. Is she the past or the present for you? She's looking lovely tonight, too—dontcha think?"

He gave me a sphinxlike smile.

"Lainie's not just a memory for you, is she, Hector?"

Silence.

Hector was such a pro. I knew I had no chance of making him say anything incriminating, but I had to give it one last try. "Did you and Lainie plan it all along? Or is she the brains and you're just the—"

*Just the what?* I didn't know how to finish the sentence without being unforgivably vulgar.

"Oh, look, Alice," he said evenly, gazing across the room. "There are the Ballingers. I must go and say hello. Excuse me, won't you?"

I walked to a table and looked for an hors d'oeuvre I hadn't tried before. I had eaten a school of smoked salmon and a thousand of the things that looked like a little bale of hay filled with hot goat cheese. Delicious, but I needed to try something new. At last I found a new treat—something full of basil and cilantro.

At ten-thirty I started saying my good-byes to each and every one I knew, and many I didn't. Everyone was now pleasantly bombed on one kind of substance or another. Fliss was holding court in the parlor and when he saw me preparing to leave grabbed me and held me captive for about twelve minutes, telling me the story of his school days in some dreary English industrial city—perhaps Sheffield. All I could glean was that it wasn't Liverpool, where, as even I knew, the Beatles came from.

When I said good-bye to Mr. Bloodworth, everyone's favorite gourmet loan shark, he eyed me up and down as if I were a London broil, and then shook my hand as if we would never see each other again. That made me nervous.

I left the brownstone and started to walk home. It was only a few blocks to my place. I walked very slowly, trying to be casual, almost sauntering.

The streets were empty. It was just a bit chilly. I buttoned the top of my jacket.

When I was half a block from my loft building I slowed down even more.

The thought came to me that this whole elaborate trap with the buttons was ridiculous . . . that I had made a fool of myself. Not the first time.

I started to fumble in my purse for the keys.

Then the garbage pail cover slammed into the wall next to my face. It hit so hard that my eardrums seemed to explode.

I staggered. The cover clattered and bounced beside me, like a pet dog.

Someone grabbed my hair and yanked my head back. I saw a man's face. I knew him but I didn't know who it was.

Something glittered in his hand. Then I realized it was a knife. I felt no fear because my head was spinning.

The man was repeating something over and over again, but I couldn't make out the words. They were like a poem or a mantra.

He brought the knife close to my throat. I felt fear then. I could understand what he was saying. I tried to scream but I couldn't.

"Murdering bitch . . . You're one of them . . . Murdering bitch . . . You're one of them." Over and over.

Suddenly Tony loomed up behind him. I could see Tony bring both fists down on the man's back. In a minute, the assailant fell to the ground beside me. The knife dropped out of his hand.

Tony started for him again.

"Stop it! Stop it!" I shouted.

Tony cursed but stopped.

"Are you okay? Should I get an ambulance?"

"No, Tony, no. Just give me a minute. I'm woozy but I'm all right."

Tony kicked the knife away.

I stared down at the moaning man, who was holding tightly to Tony's leg.

I found, to my utter astonishment, that I was looking at the gentle, lovestruck, middle-aged lawyer—Sidney Rickover.

He was the last person on earth I believed had anything to do with the murder of Niles and Penny—or the robberies.

And for some reason I felt no anger at him. None at all. Only curiosity.

I knelt beside him. "Why did you call me that?"

He glared at me, breathing hard.

"Please tell me. Why did you say I'm a murderer?"

"You and your friends—you killed her. You killed her as surely as if you had put a knife in her heart. She wasn't even supposed to be in town that week. But she was too sick to travel."

I stood up.

"What is he talking about?" Tony asked angrily.

"Get the police, Basillio."

He walked to the corner and used the pay phone. Then he hurried back. But Rickover was going nowhere.

"Do you remember what Rothwax told us, Tony? On the answering machine. About the frail old woman who had died during one of those robberies."

"Yeah, I remember."

"That was Sidney's mother. Isn't that so, Mr. Rickover?" I asked the attorney.

He nodded, tears in his eyes.

"His mother!" Tony repeated. "How do you know that?"

"Well, it had to be the mother—or grandmother or aunt or old nanny—or whatever—of someone involved in this case. Look, it really isn't that complicated, Tony. While the Collins sisters were fitting wealthy women with bridal gowns, mother of the bride gowns, and so on, darling Hector, unbeknownst to them, was looting neighboring apartments with his friend Niles. When I looked through the fashion magazines and then cross-checked the names of the women the sisters had outfitted against the telephone book, they were virtually all in the area of the robberies.

"It was easy for them to gain access, case buildings, bribe maintenance people, observe schedules, because Hector was always a part of the Collins entourage. They were stealing in order to pay back money they had borrowed from a loan shark—Brewer Bloodworth."

My head began to spin again. I held on tightly to Basillio for balance. Then it cleared.

"Rickover's friendship with Samantha enabled him to find out it was Hector and Niles who had broken into his mother's apartment and contributed to her death. I don't know how he found out—he might have hired someone, or it may have fallen into his lap, or he may have simply guessed the truth after seeing how the Collins sisters' operation worked—and then confirmed his suspicions.

"But once he knew for sure, he acted. He wasn't interested in justice. Only vengeance. He killed Niles with the almond paste. He murdered Penny because he found those buttons in her studio—he recognized them as his mother's—and believed Penny was in on the robberies. I don't think she was, necessarily, but we can't know that for certain. I think Hector gave her the buttons simply because, as Felix suggested, he couldn't fence them easily. Sidney attempted to murder me because he saw me wearing the denim vest with those buttons this evening. And if we hadn't stopped him tonight, he surely would have killed Hector, too."

I looked down at Rickover again. His eyes were closed. He looked totally and utterly crushed. "The man," I said, "might well be mad as a hatter."

A patrol car pulled up. A crowd gathered. We all went down to the precinct house. They took statements from Tony and me. They carried Sidney off to be booked. I declined medical care. Rickover, I was told, was taken to the emergency ward before being booked for an X-ray of his ribs.

Tony and I arrived back at my loft at three in the morning. In spite of our traumas, we had triumphed.

At least that's what we thought as we toasted our brilliant trap at three in the morning with my last remaining bottle of Courvoisier, a gift some months ago from Felix.

The shocker was to come six hours later. In the person of Detective Stark. The bubble of triumph burst.

# Chapter 15

Detective Stark arrived unannounced at my loft at nine A.M. He found two healthy felines and Tony and me. Tony had injured his back overpowering Sidney Rickover and was moving like a wooden soldier.

Stark refused coffee and a seat. He stood just inside the door.

"I heard about the incident last night and I read your statement," he said. Then he turned to Tony. "And I read yours as well."

I resolved to be magnanimous because I was sure he had paid me a visit to apologize for not believing that Niles had been murdered and for not doing one damn thing to help me.

But he wasn't there to apologize.

"You accuse Mr. Rickover of two separate murders in your statement. One case, of course, I'm familiar with."

"Yes, I know you are."

"The problem is . . . you provide not one damn piece of hard evidence. You spin a fine tale. It all sounds fine. But that is not the way we work. Do you have anything concrete to tie Rickover to the murders?"

"The statement contains everything I know about this case."

"Well, it isn't enough."

Tony interrupted the dialogue angrily. "Then forget the two murders! Charge the bastard with the attempted murder of Alice Nestleton. You have an eyewitness. I was there."

"That's also a problem," Detective Stark said gently.

"A problem, Detective? How could that be a problem?" I queried, suddenly very nervous.

"Well, Mr. Rickover claims that you . . . that you . . . well, solicited him."

"For what?"

"Sex. He claims you offered him a sex-for-money situation. An act of prostitution. He claims that he refused your offer, that you became upset, came after him with a garbage pail lid. He says you threatened his life. Whereupon he drew the knife in self-defense."

Tony and I stared at each other, incredulous.

"I just wanted to let you know what was happening," Stark said.

He turned to go.

"Just a minute," I said. "I want you to know, Detective, that I usually turn my tricks uptown. But Mr. Rickover was just too ripe to pass up. You know what I mean, don't you?"

Stark closed the door behind himself quietly.

I sat there on the sofa, stunned.

"Well," Tony noted, "you said last night Rickover is mad as a hatter. You were wrong, weren't you? He's crazy like a fox. That guy has some very sly moves."

"He's probably out by now."

"Probably is, Swede. And if I was Hector I would be plenty worried," Tony noted, and then very carefully lowered himself onto the sofa beside me.

It was funny. Sitting there at home—in safety—brought up in me the kind of fear of Rickover I never exhibited during the actual attack.

I felt suddenly chilled. I got a wrap and returned to the sofa. "Why didn't he kill Hector first? That would make sense. He was probably the ringleader of the robbery team. And he probably got in Rickover's way all the time with Samantha."

Tony replied: "Well, if the guy is crazy he thinks a lot of people were in Hector's gang. If he kills him outright, he'll never find out who all the others were. Look . . . he figured out that you were in the gang, too, Bloody Mama." Tony winced from the back pain as he relished his own little joke.

"No," I replied, suddenly caught up in the

strangeness of that fact—that Sidney had left the most malevolent one alone.

It was very strange. I was missing something. I was slow on the uptake. This should have occurred to me before.

Bushy ambled by. Tony grabbed at his tail . . . missed. Pancho made a run along the south wall of the loft, a blinding gray flash.

Then I continued my thought out loud: "No, he didn't have to kill Hector first. Because Hector was being watched. Hector was in a way guaranteed."

"Who was watching him?" Tony asked. Then he sat up straight. "My God! You were watching him, Swede—I mean, Alice."

"Isn't that the truth! I was *hired* to watch him."

I felt like a monumental jackass.

I leaned back and closed my eyes.

"What do we do now?" Tony asked.

A delicious, almost absurd idea bubbled up in my head. I started to laugh.

"What's so funny?"

"How would you like to do a scene with me, Tony?"

"Like in acting class?"

"Precisely."

"It's been a long time, hasn't it?"

"Well, it won't be a very hard one—or a very long one. Sort of an abbreviated *Detective Story*."

"Do I get to play Kirk Douglas?"

"He was in the movie, Tony. I'm talking about the play."

"We're both a little young to have seen that production."

"Doesn't matter. You don't have a speaking part."

"No lines! There's no end to your insults. But okay. Where do we perform? Here?"

"No, Tony. On Greene Street."

"Greene Street, eh? All right. You get old Pops, the doorman, and let's all hobble over there together."

Forty minutes later our repertory group stumbled out of the treacherous elevator. Lainie Wiegel was waiting for us, carrying Bobbin in her arms. I felt kindly toward her. When I was young I always answered the door with a feline in arms. And Big Bobbin had one of those long-suffering looks on his face, as if to say: "Do you see what I have to go through? Do you see what a wonderful cat I am? How many cats my size would let themselves be manhandled like a side of beef?"

Tony and I entered. I didn't waste any time raising the curtain on our playlet.

"Lainie, I have bad news."

She released Bobbin. Lainie folded her arms protectively in front of her, as if to ward off a blow. She turned suspicious, frightened eyes on me.

"Sidney Rickover has been arrested for

the murder of Penny Motion," I went on. "He has implicated you in the murder of your husband. He is probably using it to get a deal for himself. But he said that he saw you put the almond paste in the paté."

She didn't say a word for the longest time. She just stood there, hands folded in front of her, head slightly bowed.

"Maybe you'd better sit down, Lainie," Tony suggested.

She shook her head. Then she took an enormous breath. "I'll be right back," she said.

She went over to one of the enormous walk-in closets and vanished inside it. She came out quickly and walked over to us, carrying something in her hand.

She held it up. It was a lovely pin—a bird of paradise in sterling silver with two diamonds for eyes. No question it was valuable.

"Do you remember this?" she asked us.

Tony looked blankly at her.

"No," I said.

"This," Lainie said, "was the only piece of jewelry I was wearing that day."

She turned the pin over and over in her hands, saying nothing.

"I want to tell you the truth now," she said at last.

"I think it's important that you do that, Lainie," I said.

"Yes. The truth, Alice. All of it. I saw Sidney Rickover lift up the lid on the Cuisinart and put something in the paté that afternoon. I asked him what he was doing. He said Niles had asked him to come into the kitchen and add a little curry powder to the paté. He said it needed it little something. I thought nothing more of it."

She sat down before continuing. Her hands furiously turned the pin around and around, but her voice remained calm.

"Afterward . . . I mean, when it was discovered what had killed Niles, I confronted Sidney. I told him I was going to the police. I begged him to tell me why he would do such a horrible thing. Did he have any idea what he was doing? Was it some kind of sick joke? Or had he actually known that it would kill Niles? And for god sakes why?

"He told me that Niles was a thief and a murderer. He pointed to this pin. Said it had been stolen during a robbery on Central Park West. One of several robberies that Niles participated in. Except that an old woman died in this particular one. He told me that if I said anything to anyone, he'd make sure that I was arrested and convicted as an accomplice to the robbery and the murder. At first, when he said all that I thought he was crazy, and I told him so. But then he said he had proof. Proof that Niles and Hector were part of a robbery ring. And then he asked me if Niles had ever given me any presents. I said yes, of course. Niles often gave me things. Sidney told me to get all the jewelry I'd received from Niles. He identified every piece of it as stolen property. He told me to keep my mouth shut and do exactly as he told me, or I would go to prison, lose the loft, lose everything.

"And last of all, he said to hire you . . . to put you on Hector's trail . . . to implicate Hector in Niles's murder."

Then she began to cry. It started slowly but built up into racking sobs. There was nothing we could do for her now.

"Call Detective Stark," I instructed Tony.

There was only one other thing Tony and I did that day. With Lainie's permission we boxed Bobbin and carried him back to the Collins sisters' boutique.

Samantha was upstairs playing the harpsichord. We freed Bobbin amid the chiffon and lace and good black jersey. Julia, the salesgirl, opened the door leading up to the Collinses' living quarters. And we all watched the big old cat bound up the stairs—home. Why shouldn't he be home? Hector the thief was not going to be around for a long time.

Then Tony and I went into a Chelsea pub to celebrate. He made the toast: "To our theater company and the shortest, most effective version of *Detective Story* ever staged. And to Joseph Wiseman, a brilliant actor who was in both the stage *and* the movie production."

I had to admit, it was nice to sit and have

a drink with Basillio, just to talk over old times.

But I couldn't stay very long.

"Wait a minute, Swede!" Tony protested when I climbed off my barstool and kissed him sweetly on the cheek.

"Can't, Tony," I said. "I've got to get home."

"Why?"

"That's none of your business, Tony."

"Oh."

"Anyway, so long, Tony."

"Just a minute! Just one more drink, okay?"

"No," I said regretfully.

"Well . . . all right. But there's one question you *have* to answer before you leave."

"What's that, Tony?"

"When can I call you Swede again, Alice?"

I smiled at him. "Tony," I said, "that all depends on you."

Alice Nestleton kicks up
her heels in the next
Lydia Adamson mystery,
*A Cat in a Chorus Line,*
coming to you in
May 1996.

# Chapter 1

"I don't know why I agreed to go to this stupid party, anyway," I shouted angrily to Tony Basillio. He was rushing me. I don't like to be rushed when I'm dressing.

"One . . . we're late already, Madame Nestleton. And two . . . it's not a party."

"Then what is it?" I inquired, trying to figure out in the mirror how many buttons on my blouse I should undo. It was a sultry summer night, true enough, but three buttons were a bit risqué—given my age.

"Well, it's more like a charity ball."

I snorted. "In a Hell's Kitchen tenement? Get real, Basillio. It's an old-fashioned rent party."

"Look, Swede. The man is old and sick and broke. And he's one of ours."

"What do you mean, 'one of ours'?"

"Like us. Theater people."

As cornball as that expression was, I guess Tony had a point. If anyone was "theater people," it was Peter Nelson Krispus. During the 1970s he wrote the words and music for three strange "operettas." Two had enjoyed success "WOB"—Way Off-Broadway. One closed after four nights on Broadway. Critics either loathed Krispus or loved him. One said he set back the musical comedy form a hundred years. Another said "Krispus is delusional. He thinks he can make a bump-and-grind vaudeville show into an art form." And the prestigious critic of the *New York Times* wrote: "Krispus has made an amazing theatrical leap. He has successfully fused Gilbert and Sullivan with Eugene Ionesco."

Now there was nothing left of his genius, if that was what he had had. He no longer wrote music or anything else. His plays, or operettas, or *divertissments* (everyone had a different name for them) were no longer performed. And the memory of them was kept alive by a small cult of followers, mostly in academia. There was even, I had heard, a name for his style of theatrical piece—"operetta of the absurd."

I had seen only one Krispus production. It was called, if I remember correctly, *Ending on a Dominant.* The songs—lewd takeoffs on Gilbert and Sullivan—never quite registered, as I had only limited knowledge of Gilbert and Sullivan to begin with. The friends with whom I was sitting that night tried to induce me to leave with them at intermission. But I hung in; I saw the entire piece. And forgot it all twelve minutes after I left the theater.

"We only stay there an hour or so. It gets very crowded," Tony explained.

"When do they pass the hat?" I asked.

"No hat. Just a big flowerpot on a ledge over a walled-up fireplace. People do it discreetly."

I put the finishing touch on—my grandmother's tiny jade earrings—and began opening cans to feed Bushy and Pancho, who were getting angry at my slothfulness.

When they saw I was opening just plain old cat food cans they became angrier, because I had promised them Norwegian sardines with skin and bones intact.

"Learn to postpone gratification, boys," I cautioned them. Bushy looked ashamed of me, at my betrayal. He turned his head away. Pancho shortened his manic runs from imaginary enemies and began an almost stately trot, giving me the evil eye on occasion.

"Look at that lunatic cat," Tony said, shaking his head at Pancho's antics. "Now he thinks he's one of the Lippanzaners."

"Do not call Pancho a lunatic. I don't appreciate it."

"You would think that as he gets older he would get calmer. But not Pancho. He runs all day. He runs all night. A lot of people hope that whoever is chasing him will finally catch him."

"He was abused as a kitten."

Tony found that very funny. "If I know one thing," he said, "it's that Pancho was never a kitten. He sprang full blown and running out of his mother's womb."

"Of course he was a kitten . . . a cuddly little ball of gray. And then the world turned on him." It was a ridiculously dramatic line of soap opera idiocy. I don't know what possessed me to utter it.

Tony applauded sardonically, then said: "I think he needs a woman."

"Who?"

"Pancho."

"He's celibate."

"It would do him good. He would have to pay attention. He would have to stop and look around."

"Do you have someone in mind?"

"In fact, Madame Nestleton, I do. I don't know her name but she lives in a cellar around Twenty-ninth and Lexington."

"A cellar?"

"Yes. A cellar. I was walking past and the cellar was open and this cat was seated about three steps down. She had those big ears and a weird shape."

"You mean a Japanese Bobtail?"

"Maybe. I didn't ask her. Anyway, she had the wide eyes and spooky black pupils of cats who spend most of their lives in the dark. And she had beautiful black and white markings. And I said to myself, as we stared at each other, now this is the perfect woman for Pancho. I mean, perfect. Let's face it—Pancho isn't much to look at and this lady in the cellar probably can't see in daylight anymore. She'd only see Pancho in the dark. Which, let's face it . . . given all his scars . . . is when he looks best."

"Make the match, Tony," I said.

Then I placed the dishes of cat food down in the usual location and got back to the real matter at hand.

"What really confuses me, Tony, is why they would have this kind of rent party in late August, when all the *theater* people with any kind of money are out of the city."

"I think the date has some kind of significance. It's always on August twenty-first. Maybe it's someone's birthday. Or an anniversary."

Suddenly a wondrous breeze just floated across my loft. It was almost cool and very welcome, since my newly installed ceiling fan had broken down completely.

Both of my cats had already forgiven me, forgotten their dream of sardines, and were deep into their food.

"Actually," Tony said, "I was shocked when you finally agreed to accompany me to a Krispus party."

"You shock easy."

"Why *are* you coming?"

I grinned. "Why do you think?"

"Love and compassion for me and the desire to make me happy," Tony replied in an absolute monotone.

"Actually I want to see those cats," I corrected. I was talking about George Bernard and Shaw, as Krispus's two cats were named. They were silver tabby Maine coon cats and I just had to see if they were as big and beautiful as Tony claimed they were. Of course I knew in my heart that my red and cream Bushy was the biggest and most beautiful Maine coon cat of all times.

We took the bus uptown and got off at 49th Street and 8th Avenue. We walked west toward Krispus's apartment on 52nd Street and 10th Avenue. Tony grabbed my hand and held it tightly.

"Nostalgia?" I queried.

"Exactly."

This was indeed our old neighborhood. It was the neighborhood of virtually every young man and woman who came to New York to study acting.

Tony and I had met in an acting school over a theater on 52nd Street and Broadway. We hung out in a Greek coffee shop on 47th Street and 9th Avenue. We drank beer in a working-class bar on 50th and 8th.

It was growing darker and warmer. Tony was beginning to wax poetic: "Call it the theater district, call it the Great White Way, call it the Deuce, call it Hell's Kitchen; call it whatever you want, but it still has the highest concentration of theaters and Laundromats and junkies in the country. And I love it."

We reached the building where Krispus lived. It was a grimy six-story brownstone with a crumbling stoop.

The front door was propped open with an out-of-date telephone book—a pathetic attempt to coax a street breeze in.

The lock on the hallway door was long gone.

"They're on the fifth floor," Tony said.

Up we trudged.

"I don't hear any music," I noted as we climbed.

"How many times do I have to tell you! It's not that kind of party."

Then he kissed me on the neck and halted my ascent. Whispering dramatically, he said: "Doesn't this feel like one of those old gangster movies? A tall, beautiful, golden-haired woman climbs the stairs of a seedy West Side tenement. With her is the dark, ugly, flashily dressed killer."

"You're not flashily dressed, Tony," I noted and resumed the climb.

We reached the fifth floor. Tony led me to the front apartment and knocked.

I knew exactly what I would see when the door opened: a refrigerator. These long, narrow "railroad flats" always opened into the back of the apartment—the kitchen. In fact, I could visualize the whole scheme. There would be two large windows in the front that looked down on the street, and then no windows at all until you reach the back of the apartment. Then two more large windows in the kitchen, looking down on the yard. Off the kitchen would be the bathroom, with one tiny window. No partitions throughout. No separations. Yes, I knew these kinds of apartments. I had lived in enough of them.

The door swung open. I smiled. It *was* the kitchen.

Framed in the doorway was a heavyset woman about sixty years old with flat, wide hips and frizzy red-gray hair all over the place. Her face was dark with old freckles. She was smoking a cigarette in an elongated holder. She wore a dime-store kimono and on her feet were rubber sandals.

Tony said warmly: "You're Mrs. Krispus. Adda Krispus."

"What do you want?" the woman replied.

Then I saw the cats. They had obviously wandered into the kitchen, curious. My heart gave one of those little leaps. They were magnificent. They looked as if their mother had been a lynx and their father a snow leopard. They were huge!

"Well," mumbled a nervous and slightly embarrassed Tony, "it's always hard to be the first guests at a party."

"The party is tomorrow night," Mrs. Krispus said.

"But today is the twenty-first."

"Correct. That means tomorrow is the twenty-second. We hold the party on August twenty-second every year."

"No!" exclaimed a stubborn Tony. "On the twenty-first. I've been to them time after time, year after year."

Adda Krispus regarded Tony as if he were a difficult child. Then she grabbed both our wrists in a friendly fashion and pulled us into the apartment.

"Look around, you two! Do you see a party going on?"

To be sure, there were no other people about. The apartment was virtually empty of furniture as well. At the front end of the apartment, a man lay on a bed with wheels. He looked very old and very ill.

Tony was getting more and more embarrassed. He looked to me for help. I kept my eyes on the silver tabby Maine coons so I could describe them perfectly to Bushy.

"I'm truly sorry for busting in here like a fool," he pleaded to Mrs. Krispus.

He grasped my hand then and began to pull me toward the door.

Then a man elegantly dressed in a white linen suit walked out of the bathroom.

He stared over at us. His face was strong, compelling—but not readily identifiable as the face of a man or a woman—there was a kind of noble androgyny to it. His dyed ebony hair was slicked back. He might have been forty years old. But then again, he might just as well have been seventy.

It was a full ten seconds before I realized just who it was I was studying so minutely. The handsome man in the white suit was my old friend John Cerise.

We met years ago when I first started cat-sitting. My client was a wealthy lady on Central Park South whose passion was English shorthairs. John was then a cat show judge and breeder whose love for and knowledge of cats was proverbial. We rarely spoke to each other more than twice a year, but there was a genuine affection between us and he had a special spot in his heart for my crazy cat, Pancho, who he claimed was the reincarnation of one of Napoleon's generals.

I was delighted—if altogether mystified—at seeing John in this context. "My goodness, I can't believe this," I said, taking a step toward him. "John, what a pleasure it is to see you again. What are you doing here?"

"John? My name is not John."

I didn't know how to reply. I turned to Tony. He shrugged. I turned back to John Cerise. What was the matter with him? Had he been hit on the head?

"John, it's me . . . Alice! Alice Nestleton."

"My name isn't John," he repeated firmly.

Tony pulled at my arm and whispered, "Let's go." He said it in a weary, cynical voice, as if we had now *both* made fools of ourselves and it was time to leave.

We started to walk out.

"Wait a minute," Adda Krispus called out. We stopped.

"Look!" she said.

Look we did. In her hand now was a small pistol with a white bone handle.

She raised it, aimed, and fired it into the face of John Cerise. She fired five times. And then she dropped the weapon on the chest of the fallen man.

Adda Krispus looked at us, smiling, almost sweetly. "Shouldn't you call the police?" she inquired.

ENTER THE
MYSTERIOUS WORLD
OF
ALICE NESTLETON
IN HER
LYDIA ADAMSON
SERIES . . . BY READING
THESE OTHER
PURR-FECT CAT
CAPERS FROM SIGNET

# A CAT IN THE MANGER

Alice Nestleton, an Off-Off Broadway actress-turned-amateur sleuth, is crazy about cats, particularly her Maine coon Bushy and alley cat Pancho. Alice plans to enjoy a merry little Christmas peacefully cat-sitting at a gorgeous Long Island estate where she expects to be greeted by eight howling Himalayans. Instead, she stumbles across a grisly corpse. Alice has unwittingly become part of a deadly game of high-stakes horse racing, sinister seduction, and missing money. Alice knows she'll have to count on her catlike instincts and (she hopes!) nine lives to solve the murder mystery.

# A CAT OF A DIFFERENT COLOR

Alice Nestleton returns home one evening after teaching her acting class at the New School to find a love-struck student bearing a curious gift—a beautiful white Abyssinianlike cat. The next day, the student is murdered in a Manhattan bar and the rare cat is catnapped! Alice's feline curiosity prompts her to investigate. As the clues unfold, Alice is led into an underworld of smuggling, blackmail, and murder. Alice sets one of her famous traps to uncover a criminal operation that stretches from downtown Manhattan to South America to the center of New York's diamond district. Alice herself becomes the prey in a cat-and-mouse game before she finds the key to the mystery in a group of unusual cats with an exotic history.

# A CAT IN WOLF'S CLOTHING

When two retired city workers are found slain in their apartment, the New York City police discover the same clue that has left them baffled in seventeen murder cases in the last fifteen years—all of the murder victims were cat owners, and a toy was left for each cat at the murder scene. After reaching one too many dead ends, the police decide to consult New York's cagiest crime-solving cat expert, Alice Nestleton. What appears to be the work of one psychotic, cat-loving murderer leads to a tangled web of intrigue as our heroine becomes convinced that the key to the crimes lies in the cats, which mysteriously vanish after the murders. The trail of clues takes Alice from the secretive small towns of the Adirondacks to the eerie caverns beneath Central Park, where she finds that sometimes cat-worship can lead to murder.

# A CAT BY ANY OTHER NAME

A hot New York summer has Alice Nestleton taking a hiatus from the stage and joining a coterie of cat-lovers in cultivating a Manhattan herb garden. When one of the cozy group plunges to her death, Alice is stunned and grief-stricken by the apparent suicide of her close friend. But aided by her two cats, she soon smells a rat. And with the help of her own felinelike instincts, Alice unravels the trail of clues and sets a trap that leads her from the Brooklyn Botanical Gardens right to her own backyard. Could the victim's dearest friends have been her worst enemies?

# A CAT IN THE WINGS

Cats, Christmas, and crime converge when Alice Nestleton finds herself on the prowl for the murderer of a once-world-famous ballet dancer. Alice's close friend has been charged with the crime and it is up to Alice to seek the truth. From Manhattan's meanest streets to the elegant salons of wealthy art patrons, Alice is drawn into a dark and dangerous web of deception, until one very special cat brings Alice the clues she needs to track down the murderer of one of the most imaginative men the ballet world has ever known.

A CAT IN FINE STYLE

# A CAT WITH A FIDDLE

Alice Nestleton's latest job requires her to drive a musician's cat up to rural Massachusetts. The actress, hurt by bad reviews of her latest play, looks forward to a long, restful weekend. But though the woods are beautiful and relaxing, Alice must share the artists' colony with a world-famous quartet beset by rivalries. Her peaceful vacation is shattered when the handsome ladykiller of a pianist turns up murdered. Alice may have a tin ear, but she also has a sharp eye for suspects and a nose for clues. Her investigations lead her from the scenic Berkshire mountains to New York City, but it takes the clue of a rare breed of cats for Alice to piece together the puzzle. Alice has a good idea whodunit, but the local police won't listen, so our intrepid catlady is soon baiting a dangerous trap for a killer.

# A CAT IN A GLASS HOUSE

Alice Nestleton, after years of Off-Off Broadway, sees stardom on the horizon at last. Her agent has sent her to a chic TriBeCa Chinese restaurant to land a movie part with an up-and-coming film producer. Instead, Alice finds herself right in the middle of cats, crime, and mayhem once again. Before she can place her order, she sees a beautiful red tabby mysteriously perched amid the glass decor of the restaurant . . . and three young thugs pulling out weapons to spray the restaurant with bullets. A waitress is killed, and Alice is certain the cat is missing, too. Teamed up with a handsome, Mandarin-speaking cop, Alice is convinced the missing cat and the murder are related, and she sets out to prove it.

# A CAT WITH NO REGRETS

Alice Nestleton is on her way to stardom! Seated aboard a private jet en route to Marseilles, with her cats Bushy and Pancho beside her, she eagerly anticipates her first starring role in a feature film. To her further delight, the producer, Dorothy Dodd, has brought her three beautiful Abyssinian cats along. But on arrival in France, tragedy strikes. Before Alice's horrified eyes, the van driven by Dorothy Dodd goes out of control and crashes, killing the producer instantly. As the cast and crew scramble to keep their film project alive, Alice has an additional worry: what will happen to Dorothy's cats? As additional corpses turn up to mar the beautiful Provençal countryside, Alice becomes convinced the suspicious deaths and the valuable cats are related. She sets one of her famous traps to solve the mystery.

# A CAT ON THE CUTTING EDGE

What do you do if your beloved kitty suddenly becomes a snarling, hissing tiger when you try to coax him into his carrier for a routine trip to the vet? If you're savvy cat-sitting sleuth Alice Nestleton, you call for help from the Village Cat People, a service for cat owners with problem pets. Yet Pancho's unruliness becomes the least of Alice's worries when her Cat People representative, Martha, is found murdered at Alice's front door. Martha's friends sense foul play and ask Alice to investigate. Alice would much rather focus her attention on her new loft apartment in twisty, historic Greenwich Village. But a second murder involving the Cat People gives her "paws." When a series of clues lead Alice to a Bohemian poet and trendy New York's colorful past, the Village becomes the perfect place to catch a killer.

# A CAT ON A WINNING STREAK

Out-of-work actress Alice Nestleton is willing to go as far as Atlantic City for a gig. Relaxing in a fabulous suite, she is startled by a slinky cat crawling up to her sixteenth-floor window. Alice's quest for its owner takes her to the nasty scene of Adele Houghton slashed to death and her roommate, Carmella, standing there covered in blood. Naturally, the police nab Carmella, but her handsome lover insists she is innocent and begs Alice to find the real killer. Alice is ready to bet that the murderer did in poor Ms. Houghton in order to steal her legendary, dice-charming cat. But the odds could be longer than a cat's nine lives against Alice stopping a fast-shuffling pro from stacking the deck with one more death—which could be her own.

Lydia Adamson is the pseudonym
of a noted mystery writer
who lives in New York.

# THE DR. NIGHTINGALE MYSTERY SERIES
## BY LYDIA ADAMSON

11.

S

Sayers,
ombina-
ur with
—$4.99)

a High-
y. Cats
volume

—$4.99)

Agatha
ngaging
seaside
mystery
—$3.99)

Desires,
th, and
jug of
Alfred
s besot-
to the
—$4.99)

. Send
$15.00